"We see death all around us. Plants, animals, friends, family all die. We know, too, that we will die; but as we witness the glorious rebirth of nature in springtime, we inevitably ask ourselves, is death the ultimate and final end; does it have the last word to say about our life? . . . We may rationally reject the hope and confidence at the core of our being; it may well be a deception, the last trick, the ultimate deception of a vindictive, cruel and arbitrary universe. But the decisive religious question, perhaps the only religious question that really matters, is whether that hope which is at the center of our personality is cruel deception or whether it is a hint of an explanation, a rumor of angels, the best insight we have into what human life is all about."

ANDREW GREELEY

A RUMOR
OF ANGELS

Edited by Gail Perry and Jill Perry

BALLANTINE BOOKS • NEW YORK

Library of Congress Catalog Card Number: 89-91651

ISBN 0-345-35961-5

Manufactured in the United States of America

First Edition: November 1989

Grateful acknowledgment is made to the following for permission to reprint previously published material:

PREFACE

$\mathbf{W}$e all die, but few of us care to think much about it. So, at first glance, an inspirational book on such a grievous subject may seem incongruous. But *A Rumor of Angels* isn't entirely about death. It's about the way we choose to live in the face of death, whether our own or that of a loved one. Within these pages are the words of such literary masters and contemporary figures as Leo Tolstoy, E. B. White, Elisabeth Kübler-Ross, and Maya Angelou—all of whom gracefully express, through eloquent poetry and profound prose, the challenges, sorrows, and hopes that are death's companions. Limited neither by historical nor philosophical boundaries, these disparate voices have been gathered to form an easily accessible source of insight and comfort.

The book is divided into three chapters.

CHAPTER ONE focuses on the gift of life and the ways in which life becomes more precious as we acknowledge our finitude and the finitude of those close to us. Selected passages reflect our struggle to differentiate between what we superficially perceive to be important and what we discover to be ultimately important.

CHAPTER TWO addresses grief and its many underlying dark emotions such as guilt, anger, depression, and remorse. These passages explore the need to accept and share our human responses, for to ignore them only irritates and perpetuates inner pain.

CHAPTER THREE brings us into the light

again. Selections speak positively to those whose death is imminent, as well as to those who must learn to carry on after severe loss. They offer not a series of pat answers and clichés of comfort but real-life experiences and convictions of hope and meaning in the midst of death.

Readers will note Biblical scripture and prayers throughout *A Rumor of Angels*. Surely these quotes will be of particular interest to Christians, whose faith is rooted in the assurance that our physical death is by no means a spiritual one. But this book is *not* limited to a Christian perspective. Anyone willing to confront the inevitability of death can find a wealth of strength and understanding in the inspired words that follow.

INTRODUCTION

When the authors of **A Rumor of Angels** asked me to introduce this book, I accepted because doing so offered me the opportunity to be with a great many people as they face perhaps the most challenging crises of their lives. I have always been attracted to people in crisis and in struggle. It is then that they seem to me most beautiful. But day after day, as I thought of the subject, only the most incoherent responses came to mind, symbolizing, I think, the incoherence of one's initial approach to the subject of death, dying, and letting go.

For many years, as a child and young adult, I was intensely suicidal. Not all the time, but periodically. Life often seemed not worth living because too many tangled and unexamined bonds held me back *from* living, bonds I was afraid to dissect *ruth*lessly. (Ruth is the name of an older sister of mine to whom I was very close as a child, and I was used to having her beside me as I stared down the ogres in my life, a role which, because of the passage of time and her own life situation—with plenty of ogres of its own— she could no longer assume.) This reality just occurred to me. That it was facing disaster without my sister's support that most frightened me, and not the disaster itself.

There were three times when I was in danger of dying and felt very conscious of it. Once was when I was in a pickup truck with one of my teenage brothers who drove recklessly and turned it over on a backcountry dirt road: I wound up unscathed under the back wheels. He suffered a broken leg, and our cousin, Dorothy Mae, who was riding with us, suffered a broken leg and hip. Another time was in Jamaica during a period of psychological crisis, when I foolishly accepted a drag on a spliff offered by a smiling Jamaican "brother" on the beach and then swam far out into the water: I blacked out and would no doubt have drowned if the water had been deep. I was out for only a few seconds and was able somehow to keep my head above water and let the tide help propel me back to shore. The third time, which came between these two, occurred when I was a college student seeking an abortionist. Not having found one, and having been abandoned by my sister, who did not "believe" in abortion, I was planning to slit my wrists. It was this brush with death that makes me think that when someone mentions death, dying, and letting go, I can speak a hopeful word. For although I believe that the struggle not to die is very hard, dying itself may not be. What happened to me, once I realized forever that there was no one loving human hand holding mine (neither sister's, nor lover's), no one pair of human arms in which to seek comfort, and was therefore driven to say finally to the Universe: "Okay, let *us go*," I experienced all the warm, white light and felt all of the nonjudgmental oneness and peace of which, by now, everyone has no doubt heard.

In my life suffering has given birth to truth (I am alone, yes, but not alone) and light, and a feeling of being loved by the Universe (a part of it, and vice versa) whatever might be my "sins," shortcomings, failures, and flaws. Death itself is proof of life's imperfection, and this we share with all things. Life is life's reward; and part of life is being shown the door that leads us from the tight encirclement of our grief and into the Universe's spacious arms.*

If everything is a gift if only we could perceive it as such, then the wrappings of death, like the wrappings of grief, might conceal the one last treasure which heretofore has eluded us.

In any event I realize that if you have bought and are reading this book, or were only flipping through its pages in confusion or rage, it is because you are in the grip of loss, terror, grief, or pain. In this place there is much for you besides what you are feeling now. One day, if not at this moment, you will be able to absorb this fact. In the meantime please know I wanted to be with you to the extent that a printed page can impersonate a wish. I wanted to be for you my sister's hand.

Courage.

Alice Walker
San Francisco 1986

*The authors make a distinction between a personal God and the "Universe."

LIVING

....

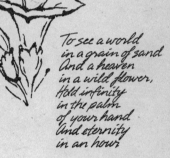

To see a world
in a grain of sand
And a heaven
in a wild flower,
Hold infinity
in the palm
of your hand
And eternity
in an hour.

—WILLIAM BARCLAY

You're an angel," blurted Jan's husband.

"An angel!" I thought angrily. How could I be an angel? I put Jan through three months of rigorous rehabilitation. Yet, within ten days from her discharge home, she collapsed. Now, after six more grueling months of hospitalization, I felt like a failure. Almost shamefully I protested, "I wish I could have done so much more! I am *no* angel."

I teach my patients "quality" living: It is the life in our years that counts and not the years in our life. I speak of the intangibles—love, inner beauty, memories—that outlast time. Do I believe it all? Jan's husband rewinds my spirit:

"You gave my wife back to me for ten days. They were such wonderful days at home. And for this I can never thank you enough."

CHAPTER ONE is about *living* and *loving*, though your own days, or the days of your loved one, may be as few as ten.

Living . . . To appreciate special moments and to maintain your spirit and character may not seem possible or even desirable when you are amid desperation. But Chapter One, in its entirety, will

3

fill you with encouragement and confidence to live fully even now.

Loving . . . To share/bear each other's burdens and to communicate honestly and openly may be a challenge beyond your strength. But Chapter One will guide the love in you to meaningful expressions and actions. Most important, the poetry and prose will assure you of the worth and foreverness of love. As inner beauty can transcend a damaged body, so can love transcend death.

*D*uration is not a test of true or false. The day of the dragon-fly or the night of the Saturnid moth is not invalid simply because that phase in its life cycle is brief. Validity need have no relation to time, to duration, to continuity.

ANNE MORROW LINDBERGH

*T*he advantage of living is not measured by length, but by use; some men have lived long, and lived little; attend to it while you are in it.

MICHEL EYQUEM DE MONTAIGNE

*W*hen you work in the hospital a lot, you do sometimes find yourself imagining how you would act in those extreme situations [of your own death]. . . . I end up hoping that I would have . . . courage manifested not in wise, comforting speeches or saintly joy in the inevitable, but in the maintenance of spirit and individuality in impossible circumstances. Not to mention humor, of whatever kind.

PERRI KLASS

*H*ope means to keep living
amid desperation
and to keep humming
in the darkness.

HENRI J. M. NOUWEN

*O*n the day of his death, when his mother came into his room in the morning, the young boy spoke his last words. She asked him what he wanted for breakfast, and his reply was, "A kiss."

SANDOL STODDARD, referring to a fourteen-year-old guest of the Hospice of Marin County, California

*H*uman beings have one great asset over all living things, and that is that they have free choice. We are not powerless specks of dust drifting around in the wind, blown by random destiny. . . . In the course of terminal illness, we can give up, we can demand attention, we can scream, we can become total invalids long before it is necessary. . . . Or we have the choice to complete our work, to function in whatever way we are capable and thereby touch many lives by our valiant struggle and our own sense of purpose in our existence.

ELISABETH KÜBLER-ROSS

*A*nd there is a Catskill eagle
in some souls that can alike
dive down into the blackest
gorges, and soar out of them
again and become invisible
in the sunny spaces.

HERMAN MELVILLE

The eagle
was believed to
renew its vigor
and youth by
flying near the
sun and then
plunging into
the water.

*W*e who lived in concentration camps can remember the men who walked through the huts comforting others, giving away their last piece of bread. They may have been few in number, but they offer sufficient proof that everything can be taken from a man but one thing: the last of human freedoms—to choose one's attitude in any given set of circumstances, to choose one's own way.

VICTOR FRANKEL

*I*t is better to light one candle than to curse the darkness.

ELEANOR ROOSEVELT

I encourage such patients to set goals that are three months, six months, and a year into the future. Sometimes they protest that they'll never live that long, but my reply is that none of us know how long we will live. In the face of that uncertainty, it is still healthy to have things to look forward to, and commitments to the future can be powerfully energizing. . . .

STEPHANIE MATTHEWS SIMONTON

*N*ow is not the time to think of what you do not have. Think of what you can do with what there is.

ERNEST HEMINGWAY, *The Old Man and the Sea*

*W*hen one door of happiness closes, another opens; but often we look so long at the closed door that we do not see the one which has been opened for us.

HELEN KELLER

*T*hus says Yahweh,
who made a way through the sea,
a path in the great waters. . . .
"See, I am doing a new deed,
even now it comes to light; can you not see it?
Yes, I am making a road in the wilderness,
paths in the wilds."

ISAIAH 43:16,19

*D*ying is a wild night and a new road.

EMILY DICKINSON

I was ever a fighter, so—one fight more,
     The best and the last!
I would hate that death bandaged my eyes, and forebore,
     And bade me creep past.
.   .   .   .
For sudden the worst turns the best to the brave,
     The black minute's at end,
And the element's rage, the fiend-voices that rave,
     Shall dwindle, shall blend,
Shall change, shall become first a peace, out of pain,
     Then a light, then thy breast,
O thou soul of my soul! I shall clasp thee again,
     And with God be the rest!

ROBERT BROWNING

"You asked me about my families. Women up here speak of their first family, their second family, their third family. Counting the baby boy I lost that first winter, I've had four families. Nine children. They're out there." I knew what she meant, the little graveyard we'd passed on the way in. . . .

"Katherine Mary, we're going to know each other very well, for many years, I hope. You'll come to understand. These big things, these terrible things, are not the important ones. If they were, how could one go on living? No, it is the small, little things that make up a day, that bring fullness and happiness to a life. Your Sergeant coming home, a good dinner, your little Mary laughing, the smell of the woods—oh, so many things, you know them yourself." She took my hand.

BENEDICT and NANCY FREEDMAN, *Mrs. Mike*

What is life? It is the flash of a firefly in the night. It is the breath of a buffalo in the winter time. It is the little shadow which runs across the grass and loses itself in the sunset.

CROWFOOT, Canadian Indian, dying words

There is not enough darkness in all the world to put out the light of one small candle. . . . In moments of discouragement, defeat or even despair, there are always certain things to cling to. Little things usually: remembered laughter, the face of a sleeping child, a tree in the wind—in fact, any reminder of something deeply felt or dearly loved. No man is so poor as not to have many of these small candles. When they are lighted, darkness goes away and a touch of wonder remains.

ARTHUR GORDON

*T*he light shines in the darkness, and the darkness has not overcome it.

JOHN 1:5

Candlelight, in the Jewish faith, symbolizes the human being. The wick is the body. The flame is the soul that strives upward.

I want to tell you about the good things
      I have experienced,
      not just the disappointments I've encountered.
The happy words I've shared,
      not the hostile outbursts.
The gentle touches I've given a friend,
      not the insensitive back I turned.
The pride I've rightly felt,
      not the boastful one-upmanship.
I need to be reminded of my personal worth,
      not to review my failures.
So help me God.

SANDRA ANN McCORMICK BROOKS

*M*y brother's death has taught me . . . how important each of us is to everyone with whom we have contact, particularly our families and friends. The grief that overwhelmed my family indicated how much meaning Joe had added to our lives. . . . I rejoice that my brother Joe strove so earnestly to be caring and to develop his great talents. But I grieve that he did not seem to value the appreciation of those around him. If he had, perhaps he would not have taken himself from us.

I have learned through Joe's death to value the contribution I make to the lives of others, and the contribution they make to my life. We have not made ourselves; we are the gift of the living God to one another.

REINE DUELL BETHANY, referring to the suicide of his brother, Joe, prominent member of the New York City Ballet

*A*nd after a long time the boy came back again. "I am sorry, Boy," said the tree, "but I have nothing left to give you—My apples are gone."

"My teeth are too weak for apples," said the boy.

"My branches are gone," said the tree. "You cannot swing on them—"

"I am too old to swing on branches," said the boy.

"My trunk is gone," said the tree. "You cannot climb—"

"I am too tired to climb," said the boy.

"I am sorry," sighed the tree. "I wish that I could give you something . . . but I have nothing left. I am just an old stump. I am sorry . . ."

"I don't need very much now," said the boy. "Just a quiet place to sit and rest. I am very tired."

"Well," said the tree, straightening herself up as much as she could, "well, an old stump *is* good for sitting and resting.
Come, Boy, sit down.
Sit down and rest."
And the boy did.

SHEL SILVERSTEIN, *The Giving Tree*

*T*o appreciate beauty;
to find the best in others;
to give one's self;
to leave the world a little better,
whether by a healthy child,
a garden patch,
or a redeemed social condition;
to have played and laughed with enthusiasm,
and sung with exultation;
to know even one life has breathed easier
because you have lived . . .
This is to have succeeded.

RALPH WALDO EMERSON

If I can stop one Heart from breaking
I shall not live in vain
If I can ease one Life the Aching
Or cool one Pain

Or help one fainting Robin
Unto his Nest again
I shall not live in Vain.

EMILY DICKINSON

"You have been my friend," replied Charlotte. "That in itself is a tremendous thing. I wove my webs for you because I liked you. After all, what's a life anyway? We're born, we live a little while, we die. A spider's life can't help being something of a mess, with all this trapping and eating flies. By helping you, perhaps I was trying to lift up my life a trifle. Heaven knows anyone's life can stand a little of that."

E. B. WHITE, *Charlotte's Web*

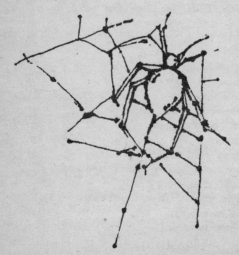

*L*ord, Make me an instrument of Thy peace.
Where there is hate, may I bring love;
Where offense, may I bring pardon;
May I bring union in place of discord; Truth,
    replacing error;
Faith, where once there was doubt; Hope, for despair;
Light, where was darkness; Joy to replace sadness.
Make me not to so crave to be loved as to love.
Help me to learn that in giving I may receive;
In forgetting self, I may find life eternal.

ST. FRANCIS OF ASSISI

*T*wo days later, in the evening, I entered her bedroom.
She was resting fairly comfortably. As was my custom, I
looked at the growing mountain of cards she received.
There was one in a red envelope, unopened. It was
addressed to me. I opened it. It said, "Happy Birthday."
By her own hand (that was obviously shaking) she had
written, "I'll always love you," and, as if she could write
no more, an almost illegible signature, "Beth." Even in
her anguish she had thought of me. She had had a nurse
get the card and then managed to write her last written
words by herself.

WILLARD K. KOHN

*D*eath is a challenge. It tells us not to waste time. . . . It tells us to tell each other right now that we love each other.

LEO F. BUSCAGLIA

The tulip—
declaration of
lasting love

*W*e call her Mrs. Fixer because she fixes
    Everything for everybody.
If you need a ride, you call her,
    Or a meal, or a telephone committee.
She'll find you an apartment or a part-time job,
    Even a date if you're in the market.
And all the time she only wants someone to love her
    But she's afraid to ask.
So she fixes everything for everybody instead
And you keep calling her when you need something
    And forget to tell her that you love her.
So she'll probably die lonely
    And have a big funeral
And everyone will tell about
    The way she fixed things all the time.

JAMES KAVANAUGH

If this day should come to an end and we don't tell you at least once that we love you, you'll be disappointed, the world will be less and we will be less.

BRENNAN MANNING

But death does not stand at the end of life, it is all through it. It is the fear of losing, the knowledge of losing that makes love tender.

BENEDICT and NANCY FREEDMAN, *Mrs. Mike*

Here death makes its greatest gift, for the sure and ever-present awareness that I shall die much sooner than I would wish, and that others are moving as quickly and surely to the same end, enhances all human relationships from that of casual acquaintance to that of deepest love. . . . If only we can learn to act as if we are going to die then death loses much of its power over us. . . . If we realize that love is stronger than death, we may see that length of life is not important.

BETTY R. GREEN and DONALD P. IRISH

*M*y father looked at a bird lying on its side against the curb near our house.

"Is it dead, Papa?" I was six and could not bring myself to look at it.

"Yes," I heard him say in a sad and distant way.

"Why did it die?"

"Everything that lives must die."

"Everything?"

"Yes."

"You too Papa? And Mama?"

"Yes."

"And me?"

"Yes," he said. Then he added in Yiddish, "But may it be only after you live a long and good life, my Asher."

I could not grasp it. I forced myself to look at the bird. Everything alive would one day be as still as that bird?

"Why?" I asked.

"That's the way the Ribbono Shel Olom made His world, Asher."

"Why?"

"So life would be precious, Asher.

Something that is yours forever is never precious!"

CHAIM POTOK,
My Name is Asher Lev

He was harsh and visibly angry with us—not because he was dying, but because he felt that we were not "living." He told us that we looked at him and thought "this poor young man is dying," while we ignored the fact that we *too* were dying. He told us that he was the only one around who was truly alive, aware of the preciousness of each moment.

LISL MARBURG GOODMAN, PH.D.

If one truly grasped all of this, what would the consequences be? . . . The radical uncertainty of death . . . makes the moment precious and therefore beautiful. It can free us from procrastination, the illusion that we have an infinite amount of time, that we can put off living until some future time—after graduation, or after career and financial security are obtained, or after a particular project is finished, or after a special relationship is established. . . . Earnest thought about one's own death does not make one fearfully or morbidly preoccupied with death, for earnestness makes one realize that time is too precious to be spent being morbid. It does not lead to a giving up of plans or projects, though it does change the mental frame of reference within which they are chosen and worked on. It does not mean one lives every day *simply* as if it were one's last—a kind of crazy living "for the moment" rather than living "in the moment". . . . To live "in the moment" means to be gracefully present to the simplest and most complex joys and tasks. It means to value the "dailiness of life."

MARCUS BORG

*S*itting in a graveyard you involuntarily cast your mind back over all your past life, your past actions, and your plans for the future. And here you do not lie to yourself as you do so often in life, because you feel as if all those people sleeping the sleep of peace around you were somehow still present, and you were conversing with them. Sitting in a graveyard you momentarily rise above your daily ambitions, cares and emotions—you rise for an instant even above yourself.

ALEXANDER SOLZHENITSYN

*F*requently in my Pursuits of whatever Kind,
let this come into my Mind;
"How much shall I value this on my Death Bed?"

JONATHAN EDWARDS, from his diary

*I*n my happier days I used to remark on the aptitude of the saying, "When in life we are in the midst of death." I have since learnt that it's more apt to say, "When in death we are in the midst of life."

A BELSEN SURVIVOR

*H*e who would teach men to die would teach them to live.

MICHEL EYQUEM DE MONTAIGNE

I had to drown kittens once, and I saw them push to stay alive. This biological push to stay alive is in me, and that's what makes me feel that I am afraid. But I also feel that life without death is meaningless. It's like a picture without a frame.

JOHN A. WHEELER

*P*art of the totality of our lives is the not-yet-existing, which includes death.

LISL MARBURG GOODMAN, PH.D.

*a*nd now you are and i am now and we're
a mystery which will never happen again,
a miracle which has never happened before—
and shining this our now must come to then

e. e. cummings

I'll remember you
And I'm sorry that the time we have is almost through
But the special thing that means so much
Is knowing we can really touch. . . .

RANDY STONEHILL

I have known thee all the time.

JOHN GREENLEAF WHITTIER, last words, to his niece

"*A*re you getting well?"

"No," Emma said. "I have a million cancers. I can't get well."

"Oh, I don't know what to do," Teddy said . . .

"Well, both of you better make some friends," Emma said. "I'm sorry about this, but I can't help it. I can't talk to you too much longer either, or I'll get too upset. Fortunately we had ten or twelve years and we did a lot of talking, and that's more than a lot of people get. . . ."

When they came to hug her, Teddy fell apart and Tommy remained stiff.

"Tommy, be sweet," Emma said. "Be sweet, please. Don't keep pretending you dislike me. That's silly."

"I *like* you," Tommy said, shrugging tightly.

"I know that, but for the last year or two you've been pretending you hate me," Emma said. "I know I love you more than anybody in the world except your brother and sister, and I'm not going to be around long enough to change my mind about you. But you're going to live a long time, and in a year or two when I'm not around to irritate you you're going to remember that I read you a lot of stories and made you a lot of milkshakes and allowed you to goof off a lot when I could have been forcing you to mow the lawn."

Both boys looked away, shocked that their mother's voice was so weak.

"In other words, you're going to remember that you love me," Emma said. "I imagine you'll wish you could tell me that you've changed your mind, but you won't be able to, so I'm telling you now I already know you love me, just so you won't be in doubt about that later. Okay?"

"Okay," Tommy said quickly, a little gratefully.

LARRY McMURTRY, *Terms of Endearment*

if there are any heavens my mother will (all by herself)
have one.

e. e. cummings

TO MY DEAR AND LOVING HUSBAND

If ever two were one, then surely we.
If ever man were lov'd by wife, then thee.
If ever wife was happy in a man,
Compare with me ye women if you can.
I prize thy love more than whole mines of gold,
Or all the riches that the East doth hold.
My love is such that Rivers cannot quench,
Nor ought but love from thee, give recompense.
Thy love is such I can no way repay,
The heavens reward thee manifold, I pray.
Then while we live, in love let's so persevere,
That when we live no more, we may live ever.

ANNE BRADSTREET

*M*any waters cannot quench love, Nor will rivers
overflow it. . . .

SONG OF SOLOMON 8:7

*L*ove is the only thing that we can carry with us
when we go. . . .

LOUISA MAY ALCOTT, *Little Women*

*H*e went before she did.
She thought she would break.
She felt she was fallin' apart.
But still she remembers
The last words he said
As he held her hand close to his heart,

"I'm gonna hold on to you
Till the moon flies away
Till the sky isn't blue,
I'm gonna hold on to you
Till the angels come call
Till the truth isn't true,
I'm gonna hold on to you."

WILLY WELCH

Til the moon flies away

*I*t should be my wishing, That I might die with kissing.

BEN JOHNSON

*though love be a day
and life be nothing,
it shall not stop
kissing*

*B*ut true love is a durable fire,
    In the mind ever burning.
Never sick, never old, never dead,
    From itself never turning.

SIR WALTER RALEIGH

*L*ove is patient, love is kind . . . bears all things, believes
all things, hopes all things, endures all things. Love never
fails . . .
. . . .
And now these three remain: faith, hope and love. But the
greatest of these is love.

I CORINTHIANS 13:4,7,13

I remember those long, early morning walks we took
together. We were both filled with a new awareness. We
gloried in the smell of grass newly mown. We laughed to
think that we had never really listened to the birds singing.
Nothing and no one was ugly to us because this was life,
and whatever came later, we had realized that what we had
together was special and it could never be taken from us.

As the cancer grew within me, my body became
misshapen and ugly, but it didn't make any difference to
you. You said, "I love what you are and that makes you
always beautiful to me." Then I realized how foolish I was
and fell asleep with a smile on my face because your love
did not waver.

BETH, cancer patient quoted by ELISABETH KÜBLER-ROSS

Love is most nearly itself
When here and now cease to matter.

T. S. ELIOT

What is REAL?" asked the Rabbit one day.

"Real isn't how you are made," said the Skin Horse. "It's a thing that happens to you. When a child loves you for a long, long time, not just to play with, but REALLY loves you, then you become Real."

"Does it hurt?" asked the Rabbit.

"Sometimes," said the Skin Horse, for he was always truthful. "When you are Real you don't mind being hurt."

"Does it happen all at once, like being wound up," he asked, "or bit by bit?"

"It doesn't happen all at once," said the Skin Horse. "You become. It takes a long time . . . Generally, by the time you are Real, most of your hair has been loved off, and your eyes drop out and you get loose in the joints and very shabby. But those things don't matter at all, because once you are Real you can't be ugly, except to people who don't understand."

MARGERY WILLIAMS, *The Velveteen Rabbit*

I think God has planned the strength and beauty of youth to be physical. But the strength and beauty of age is spiritual. We gradually lose the strength and beauty that is temporary so we'll be sure to concentrate on the strength and beauty which is forever.

J. ROBERTSON McQUILKIN

Goodbye," said the fox. "And now here is my secret, a very simple secret: It is only with the heart that one can see rightly; what is essential is invisible to the eye."

ANTOINE DE SAINT-EXUPÉRY, *The Little Prince*

I gazed at her intently and saw that those eyes, which a few days ago were smiling like lips and moving like the wings of a nightingale, were already sunken and glazed with sorrow and pain. Her face, that had resembled the unfolding, sunkissed leaves of a lily, had faded and become colorless. . . . Her neck, that had been a column of ivory, was bent forward as if it no longer could support the burden of grief in her head.

All these changes I saw in Selma's face, but to me they were like a passing cloud that covered the face of the moon and makes it more beautiful.

KAHLIL GIBRAN, *The Broken Wings*

*B*eauty here is not a matter of tidy appearances, logical properties, or even of physical prowess. Rather, it pertains to those exchanges between people, living and dying, who value one another as vessels of a purer and a more lasting force. . . .

SANDOL STODDARD

*T*he jagged, ugly cancer sore went no deeper than my flesh. There was no cancer in my Spirit.

THOMAS A. DOOLEY

28

*T*herefore we do not lose heart, but though our outer man is decaying, yet our inner man is being renewed day by day. . . . for the things which are seen are temporal, but the things which are not seen are eternal.

II CORINTHIANS 4:16,18

*P*rostrate, self-scorning,
Wingless and mourning,
Dust in the dust,
We lie as we must;
Empty. To dare not,
Know not and care not
Is our employ.
God, do Thou dower us,
Kindle, empower us,
Give us Thy joy.
Impotence clings—
How shall we bear it?
Wings, give us wings,
Wings of the spirit!

DMITRY MEREZHKOVSKY, "Prayer For Wings"

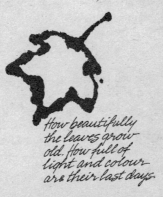

How beautifully
the leaves grow
old. How full of
light and colour
are their last days.

—JOHN BURROUGHS

I am 78—and at my age I find that I have now taken in more than 1,000 tons of water, food, and air, the chemistry of which is temporarily employed for different lengths of time as hair, skin, flesh, bone, blood, etc., then progressively discarded. I weighed in at 7 pounds, and I went on to 70, then 170, and even 207 pounds. Then I lost 70 pounds, and I said, "Who was that 70 pounds?—because here I am. . . .

I am certain that I am not the avoirdupois of the most recent meals I have eaten, some of which will become my hair, only to be cut off twice a month. This lost 70 pounds of organic chemistry obviously wasn't "me," nor are any of the remaining presently associated atoms "me." We have been making a great error in identifying "me" and "you" as these truly transient and, ergo, sensorially detectable chemistries. . . . The only difference manifest between weight before and after death is that caused by air exhaled from the lungs. . . .

Whatever life is, it doesn't weigh anything.

BUCKMINSTER FULLER

*M*ethinks my body is but the less of my better being.

HERMAN MELVILLE, *Moby Dick*

*O*ne night I thumbed through the day's mail. I noticed a postcard sent by my best friend. He had written one word on the postcard, scrawled in big letters: LIVE. Whenever I was tempted to harm myself I would look at that word and repeat it again and again and again: Live! Live! Live! I began to believe that I was not my body—*I was me.*

ROBERT VENINGA

*F*or so long my self-image depended on my physical strength and fitness. Now I'm being forced to far deeper dimensions. Never apologize for being who you are—even now. Never, never, never, never—it is a sin of the first order. No apologies. No excuses. No regrets. No complaints.

TIM HANSEL, *You Gotta Keep Dancin'*

*B*lessed are those who heal us of self-despisings. Of all services which can be done to man, I know of none more precious.

WILLIAM HALE WHITE

I cried a tear
You wiped it dry
I was confused
You cleared my mind
I sold my soul
You bought it back for me
And helped me out
And gave me dignity
Somehow you needed me.

You held my hand
When it was cold
When I was lost
You took me home
You gave me hope
When I was at the end
And turned my lies
Back into truth again
You even called me friend.

RANDY GOODRUM

"*K*now deep down that you're worth any trouble you cause."
  "You never told me that before." Peg's face cracks, into tiny pieces of stained glass, each piece glistening with moisture. . . .

MEG WOODSON, referring to her twelve-year-old daughter, Peggy, sufferer of cystic fibrosis

Compassion means to lay a bridge over to the other without knowing whether he wants to be reached.

HENRI J. M. NOUWEN

A trauma can do one of two things: It can drive your family apart if you close communication and build walls, or it can pull your family closer together if you open communication lines and build bridges of love between one another.

PAM W. VREDVELT

But for me, fear is today and dying is now. You slip in and out of my room, give me medications and check my blood pressure. Is it because I am a student nurse, myself, or just a human being, that I sense your fright? And your fear enhances mine. Why are you afraid? I am the one who is dying!

I know, you feel insecure, don't know what to say, don't know what to do. But please believe me, if you care, you can't go wrong. Just admit that you care.

ANONYMOUS

It is hoped that . . . our next generation of children will never again have to see a sign, "No Children Under Age 14 Allowed in the Hospital." It is hoped that all the children of our next generation will be permitted to face the realities of life. It is hoped that we will not "protect" them as a reflection of our own fears and our own anxieties!

ELISABETH KÜBLER-ROSS

*R*emember: the child has experienced the worst possible tragedy. She should feel terrible. If she is sent off to summer camp to forget and deny, she will not learn that she can, in fact, tolerate and overcome emotional catastrophes. Permitting the child to feel the loss when she is ready will increase her coping ability for the rest of her life.

DR. ROBERTA TEMES

*T*he worst torment was the lie, this lie that for some reason was accepted by everyone, that he was only sick, and not dying. . . . He suffered because no one was willing to admit what everyone, including himself, could see very clearly. He suffered because they lied and forced him to take part in this deception. This lie that was being told on the eve of his death, this lie that degraded the formidable and solemn act of his death . . . had become horribly painful to Ivan Ilyich.

LEO TOLSTOY, *The Death of Ivan Ilyich*

*I*t's easier to kill a man than to break the news that he is going to die.

ELIE WIESEL, *Dawn*

This is what youth must
    figure out:
Girls, love, and living.
The having, the not having,
The spending and giving,
And the melancholy time of
    not knowing.

This is what age must learn
    about:
The ABC of dying.
The going, yet not going,
The loving and leaving.
And the unbearable
    knowing and knowing.

E. B. WHITE

Let us not forget that in the nineteenth century, death
. . . had become an occasion for the most perfect union
between the one leaving and those remaining behind. The
last communion with God and/or with others was the
great privilege of the dying. For centuries there was no
question of depriving them of this privilege. But when the
lie was maintained to the end, it eliminated this
communion and its joys.

PHILIPPE ARIÈS

If someone is dying and those around them insist that they
do not die, the person dies in isolation, alone and without
the love that can offer such support and such a sense of
completion. . . .
. . . .
Truly, you can't go through the door with her, but you
can accompany her more fully to the threshold.

STEPHEN LEVINE

Hope means that at the end I will not be rejected.

ELISABETH KÜBLER-ROSS

*E*ven if death need not be welcomed, it need not always be opposed. But to stop the battle does not mean to abandon the patient or to cease caring for the patient. Caring continues even when the patient is allowed to die.

JAMES CHILDRESS

*T*he nearest friends can go
With anyone to death, comes so far short
They might as well not try to go at all.
No, from the time when one is sick to death,
One is alone, and he dies alone.
Friends make pretence of following to the grave,
But before one is in it, their minds are turned
And making the best of their way back to life
And living people, and things they understand.

ROBERT FROST

*T*hus says the Lord . . . "Does a woman forget her baby at the breast,
or fail to cherish the son of her womb?
Yet even if these forget,
I will never forget you.
Behold, I have inscribed you on the palms of my hands. . . ."

. . . .

"And you know that I am with you always; yes, to the end of time."

ISAIAH 49:15, MATTHEW 28:20

As I once died, you too must pass away.
But trust my singing promise as your own.
My melody shall sound above the fray
Of battlefields: you shall not die alone.

CALVIN MILLER, *The Finale*

Living and dying isn't easy. I'd like to see fewer courses
and lectures (including my own) and see more painful waits
beside the bed, more agonizing silences in the waiting
room. . . .

JOHN LANGONE

There was silence for a long time. I held her hand. It was
hard and soft and brittle. After a while she looked at me
again.

"I guess I'm going to leave," she said.

"I know," I said.

"I'm very tired."

"I know," I said again.

"I never died before," she smiled again a little bit.

"I've never been with someone who died before," I
said.

"I think we'll make it, Pastor." She was almost
whispering. She squeezed my hand a little.

"Will you listen while I pray?" Her eyes closed. I did
not answer. She knew what I would say.

"My Father," she whispered, "take me home because of
my Jesus, and Father, take care of this good boy here. He
has given love, and he has been my friend. Amen."

TED SCHROEDER

A friend loves at all times, and a brother is born for adversity.

PROVERBS 17:17

*C*ommunion between men (in infantry battalions) is as profound as any between lovers. Actually, it is more so. . . . It is, unlike marriage, a bond that cannot be broken by a word, by boredom or divorce, or by anything other than death. Sometimes even that is not strong enough. Two friends of mine died trying to save the corpses of their men from the battlefield. Such devotion, simple and selfless, the sentiment of belonging to each other, was the one decent thing we found in a conflict otherwise notable for its monstrosities.

PHILIP CAPUTO, referring to the Vietnam War

*S*hared suffering, shared fear make a stronger bond than blood. Pain cracks us wide open and is totally revealing, and this is when we learn what we really love and this is what we never forget.

AGNES DE MILLE

Honeysuckle—
symbol of
bonds of love.

Love is what you've been through with somebody.

JAMES THURBER

They say that the tree of loving
grows on the Bank of the River of Suffering.

PETER YARROW

Our love is
the unfolding
miracle

that expands
our joy
to include
our pain

ALLA BOZARTH-CAMPBELL, PH.D.

She and I are two unhappy ones who keep together and
carry our burdens together, and in this way unhappiness is
changed to joy, and the unbearable becomes bearable.

VINCENT VAN GOGH

The talk broke over Penny in a torrent. The relief of words washed and cleansed a hurt that had been in-growing. He listened gravely, nodding his head from time to time. He was a small staunch rock against which their grief might bear. When they finished and fell quiet, he talked of his own losses. It was a reminder that no man was spared. What all had borne, each could bear. He shared their sorrow, and they became a part of his, and the sharing spread their grief a little, by thinning it.

MARJORIE KINNAN RAWLINGS, *The Yearling*

Rejoice with those who
    rejoice;
mourn with those who
    mourn.

ROMANS 12:15

Bear one another's
    burdens,
and thus fulfill the law of
    Christ.

GALATIONS 6:2

My mother was very happy as I sat by her. But I think she knew death was near, for she said strange things to me—things touching the emotions that she would never have dared say otherwise, for affection between parents and children was never shown among my people. She called me "my daughter"—a thing she had never said before in her life.

AGNES SMEDLEY

*M*an's feelings are always purest and most glowing in the hour of meeting and of farewell.

JEAN PAUL RICHTER

I knew she was dying . . . the little sister, the younger one. . . .

Margaret was going, but out of her loss and mine I had found her again, and she me. I thought of her in my quiet as I lay waiting. Did she [think of] me as she lay gazing at the bare branches of her garden in Maryland, so far away. . . . And as I lay, staring at the October apartment fronts opposite, did the same memories come back to both? Probably, because we were sisters again.

And because we had time once more, as when we were young.

AGNES DE MILLE

*M*any bad spots in our best times, many good ones in our worst. . . . It is incredible how much happiness, even how much gaiety, we sometimes had together after all hope was gone. How long, how tranquilly, how nourishingly, we talked together that last night!

C. S. LEWIS

O, but they say the tongues of dying men
Enforce attention like deep harmony.
Where words are scarce they are seldom spent in vain,
For they breathe truth that breathe their words in pain.

WILLIAM SHAKESPEARE, *Richard II*

*W*hen a man is dying his words are worth listening to.

TSENG TZU

*T*o be with a person who is dying, to share consciousness with him, and to help him die consciously is one of the most exquisite manifestations of the Bodhisattva role.

BABA RAM DASS

*T*he book on death, dying, life, after-life is in progress. We're taking home a paperback about the death of a cat. Perhaps it is lighter reading for the evening. No doubt it is insightful, for pets are often one's introduction to the story of separation.

A young woman and man pass us. Their walk is assured and high-spirited, as if to oppose the oncoming night and stillness of town activity. Three cats of grand character trail them. They follow at a respectable distance of one to two cat-lengths from each other. Their long-haired beauty is such that it would seem an offense not to acknowledge their presence. So, we stop for a while and watch, like tourists, the happy parade.

We no sooner turn to go on our way than a sudden screech and a heavy thump strike us like a whip to the back. The hindmost cat has been hit! Hit and run over with no warning, no mercy! Head to the street, its legs claw the air. Its nose and mouth give blood, eyes grow wider and wilder. The other cats close in. Only inches away, they watch the disjointed dance of death.

The young woman covers her mouth, screams a defiant No! Her eyes strain forward, but her legs are limp. The man races to the car. Yelling through the window, he insists the driver take their pet to the doctor—hospital—clinic—or somewhere *else*. He then straightens, businesslike, but remains distant. Why is he, why is she so far away? Far away from each other and far away from their cat, no longer clawing but breathing like a pump up and down. What do they fear? The ugliness of death—as if the misshapen body means their cat is suddenly a stranger? The guilt of death—as if the accident means they failed to be all-caring and protecting? Or the pronouncement of death—as if words would release a primordial curse on all of life?

So, they stand separated. Only the cats are near to each other, seeming to react honestly. If they had hands and arms they would probably pick up and stroke the dying cat in its last moments of life. What they do, instinctively, is to be close, very close, and help their friend not to die alone.

GAIL PERRY and JILL PERRY

42

Only by drawing close to the dying, only by not fleeing death, can we discover what each Ivan Ilych needs. That need may be for silence, for talk, for the freedom to weep or rage, for the touching of hands in wordless communication. That need may be, and often is, to be allowed to be a baby again. We can make ourselves available to be used as they wish to use us, but we cannot teach the dying how to die. If we are there, however, and if we are paying careful attention, they will teach us.

JUDITH VIORST

This is indeed a place of meeting. Physical and spiritual, doing and accepting, giving and receiving, all have to be brought together. . . . The dying need the community, its help and fellowship. . . . The community needs the dying to make it think of eternal issues and to make it listen. . . . We are debtors to those who can make us learn such things as to be gentle and to approach others with true attention and respect.

DR. CICELY SAUNDERS

The most important thing any of us can do to comfort the grieving is to listen when they want to talk—and to accept their silence if they are unable to speak about their loss.

SUSAN JACOBY

*M*ost of us know how to say nothing, but few of us know when.

WES IZZARD

*I*t is no secret that many of our suggestions, advice, admonitions, and good words are often offered in order to keep distances rather than to allow closeness. . . . An old lady once told the following story:

I was so happy when one day a nice young student came to visit me and we had such a marvelous time. I told her about my husband and my children and how lonely and sad I often feel. And when I was talking, tears came out of my eyes, but inside I felt glad that someone was listening. But then—a few days later the student came back to me and said: "I have thought a lot about what you told me and about how you feel . . . and I wonder if you might be interested in joining this club that we are having. . . ." When I heard her saying this I felt a little ashamed, since I had caused so many worries for this good person, whereas the only thing I wanted was someone to listen and to understand.

HENRI J. M. NOUWEN and WALTER J. GAFFNEY

*F*inding solutions to problems is actually less important than affirming your love and concern. The greatest gift that you can give to a troubled individual is your presence. For it is the kind word that diminishes the pain, rekindles the hope, and finally generates a feeling of strength.

ROBERT VENINGA

*J*erry Cook spoke to the congregation, saying: "Many of you know that John and Pam were expecting a baby. That baby is now with the Lord. . . . Now listen to me and listen well. . . . They don't need any 'words from God' or 'inspired exhortations,' or advice. They just need you to love them and hug them and let them work through their grief. There will be a point where sympathy will no longer be needed or wanted, so please be sensitive to them and just allow them to be themselves."

PAM W. VREDVELT

*T*he older children felt the loss more deeply and for a longer period of time. . . . one day about a year after Beth died I had been to the cemetery and I came back feeling rather sad and lonely. I asked the girls if they ever went to the gravesite. They all answered that they did not. I am afraid I reacted very badly, making statements that never should have been said. Finally, the oldest girl, through tear-stained eyes, snapped at me, "You grieve any way you want, but we do not have to look at a grave to remember how much we miss and love Mother." They were right, and I have never questioned their method of expressing their grief again.

WILLARD K. KOHN

People often feel uncomfortable talking with the bereaved, because they are afraid of saying the wrong thing. Their fears are well-founded; according to a recent survey, 80% of the statements made to mourners were perceived as unhelpful. These included expressions of advice and interpretation: You shouldn't question God's will; You've got to get out more; Stop feeling sorry for yourself. . . . In contrast, *questions*, though infrequent, were felt to be helpful: Have you decided upon who should be pallbearers? How can I be of help? *Responses* that paid attention to what a person was experiencing often communicated the most understanding, acceptance and respect: It must be very painful for you; Tell me how you're feeling; Go ahead and grieve [italics added]. . . .

BEVERLY McLEOD

Amy was a young artist who lived next door to me in East Lansing, Michigan. After her mother died in November, she lived alone with her father. On Mother's Day, six months after her mother's death, I saw Amy out in the yard cutting flowers. I walked over and said, "Hi, I just thought I'd come over and talk for a while. I know that it's your first Mother's Day without your mother, and you're probably feeling unhappy."

Tears came into Amy's eyes as she blurted out an immediate response to my words. "You're the first person all day who has even mentioned Mother's Day," she exclaimed. "Doesn't anyone know that it's Mother's Day and that I miss her?" . . . Her tears were appreciative tears. Someone was finally paying attention to the sad feelings and memories already stirring inside.

ANN KAISER STEARNS, *Living Through Personal Crisis*

Now no joy but lacks salt
That is not dashed with
      pain
And weariness and fault;
I crave the stain

Of tears, the aftermark
Of almost too much
      love,
The sweet of bitter bark
And burning clove.

ROBERT FROST

Had you restrained your love, you would be free of
sorrow. The greater the love, while one possesses it, the
greater the sorrow when one is deprived of it.

VON TEPL

If it isn't just a meaningless form of words, I suppose my
heart broke that night. It really means, though, loving past
all measure.

.   .   .   .

For it had been death in love, not death of love. Love can
die in many ways, most of them far more terrible than
physical death. . .

SHELDON VANAUKEN

I can bear to die—I cannot bear to leave her—Oh, Brown,
I have coals of fire in my breast. It surprises me that the
human heart is capable of containing and bearing so much
misery.

JOHN KEATS, *letter to Charles Brown*

47

*T*o love at all is to be vulnerable. Love anything, and your heart will certainly be wrung and possibly be broken. If you want to make sure of keeping it intact, you must give your heart to no one, not even to an animal. . . . It will not be broken; it will become unbreakable, impenetrable, irredeemable.

C. S. LEWIS

*T*he great tragedy of life is not that men perish, but that they cease to love.

W. SOMERSET MAUGHAM

*W*hat is hell? I maintain that it is the suffering of being unable to love.

FYODOR DOSTOEVSKY

*O*ne has to embrace the world like a lover. One has to accept pain as a condition of existence. One has to court doubt and darkness as the cost of knowing. One needs a will stubborn in conflict, but apt always to total acceptance of every consequence of living and dying.

MORRIS L. WEST, *The Shoes of the Fisherman*

*T*ell me how much you know of the sufferings of your fellow men and I will tell you how much you have loved them.

HELMUT THIELICKE

I hold it true, whate'er befall;
    I feel it, when I sorrow most;
    'Tis better to have loved and lost
Than never to have loved at all.

ALFRED, LORD TENNYSON

*L*et me come in where you sit weeping,—aye,
Let me, who have not any child to die,
Weep with you for the little one whose love
    I have known nothing of.

The little arms that slowly, slowly loosed
Their pressure round your neck; the hands you used
To kiss.—Such arms—such hands I never knew.
    May I not weep with you?

Fain would I be of service—say something,
Between the tears, that would be comforting,—
But ah! so sadder than yourselves am I,
    Who have no child to die.

JAMES WHITCOMB RILEY

*P*ains of love be sweeter far
Than all other pleasures are.

JOHN DRYDEN

SHE DWELT AMONG THE UNTRODDEN WAYS

She dwelt among the untrodden ways
    Beside the springs of Dove,
A maid whom there were none to praise
    And very few to love.

A violet by a mossy stone
    Half hidden from the eye!
Fair as a star, when only one
    Is shining in the sky.

She lived unknown, and few could know
    When Lucy ceased to be;
But she is in her grave, and, oh,
    The difference to me!

WILLIAM WORDSWORTH

Nothing reopens the springs of love so fully as absence,
and no absence so thoroughly as that which must needs be
endless.

ANTHONY TROLLOPE

Stopped, his turning
Growth in time.
Forever now eighteen,
Forever muscled,
Mustached, moving
In our remembering minds.
Forever budding, burgeoning
His art, his thought, his life,
Never to unfold in flower
Or reach the summertime of fruit.

LOLLY QUINONES

"*H*e wasn't my flesh and blood," said the Captain, looking at the fire—"I ain't got none—but somewhat of what a father feels when he loses a son, I feel in losing Wal'r. For why?" said the Captain. "Because it ain't one loss but a round dozen. Where's that there young school boy with the rosy face and curly hair, that used to be as merry in this here parlour, come round every week, as a piece of music. Gone down with Wal'r. Where's that there fresh lad, that nothing couldn't tire nor put out, and that sparkled up and blushed so when we joked him about Heart's Delight, that he was beautiful to look at? Gone down with Wal'r. Where's that there man's spirit, all afire, that wouldn't see the old man hove down for a moment, and cared nothing for itself? Gone down with Wal'r. It ain't one Wal'r. There were a dozen Wal'r that I knowed and loved, all holding round his neck when he went down, and they're a-holding round mine now.

CHARLES DICKENS, *Dombey and Son*

*S*omehow she made possible for me my truest affections, as an act of great literature would bestow upon its devoted reader. And I have known that moment with her we would all like to know, the moment of saying, "Yes. This is what it is." An act of knowing that certifies love. I have known that. I have known any number of such moments with her, known them even at the instant they occurred. And now. And, I assume, I will know them forever.

RICHARD FORD, *My Mother, In Memory*

*M*emories are little stabs around the heart.
It's hard to lose a friend!

JAMES KAVANAUGH

Six years have already passed since my friend went away from me. . . . If I try to describe him here, it is to make sure that I shall not forget him. To forget a friend is sad. Not everyone has had a friend.

ANTOINE DE SAINT-EXUPÉRY, *The Little Prince*

forget-me-not

The heart that has truly loved never forgets.

THOMAS MORE

I don't like reminiscing
Nostalgia is not my forte
I don't spill tears
On yesterday's years
But honesty makes me say
You were a precious pearl
How I loved to see you shine,
You were the perfect girl.
And you were mine.
For a time.
For a time.
Just for a time.

MAYA ANGELOU

*E*verybody needs his memories. They keep the wolf of insignificance from the door.

SAUL BELLOW

*T*here are places I remember
all my life, though some have changed
Some forever, not for better
Some are gone and some remain
All these places have their meanings
with lovers and friends I still can recall
Some are dead and some are living
In my life I've loved them all.

JOHN LENNON and PAUL McCARTNEY

I am part of all that I have met.

ALFRED, LORD TENNYSON

*N*o love, no friendship can cross the path of our destiny without leaving some mark on it forever.

FRANÇOIS MAURIAC

*T*he "loved object is not gone," psychoanalyst Karl Abraham writes, "for now I carry it within myself. . . ." And while surely he overstates—the touch is gone, the laugh is gone, the promise and possibilities are gone, the sharing of music and bread and bed is gone, the comforting joy-giving flesh-and-blood presence is gone—it is true nonetheless that by making the dead a part of our inner world, we will in some important way never lose them.

JUDITH VIORST

I don't ask for your pity, but your understanding—no, not even that—no. Just for your recognition of me in you. . . .

TENNESSEE WILLIAMS

*E*ven the death of friends will inspire us as much as their lives. . . . Their memories will be encrusted over with sublime and pleasing thoughts, as monuments of other men are overgrown with moss; for our friends have no place in the graveyard.

HENRY DAVID THOREAU

She drew near and asked one of them whose grave it was. The child answered that that was not its name; it was a garden—his brother's. It was greener, he said, than all the other gardens. . . . When he had done speaking, he looked at her with a smile, and kneeling down and nestling for a moment with his cheek against the turf, bounded merrily away.

CHARLES DICKENS, *The Old Curiosity Shop*

Stranger call this not a place
Of fear and gloom,
To me it is a pleasant spot
It is my husband's tomb.

—CHARLES L. WALLIS

No really great song can ever attain full purport till long after the death of its singer—till it has accrued and incorporated the many passions, many joys and sorrows, it has itself aroused.

WALT WHITMAN

In the dark immensity of night
I stood upon a hill and watched
        the light
Of a star,
Soundless and beautiful and far.

A scientist standing there with
        me
Said, "It is not the star you see,
But a glow
That left the star light years ago."

Men are like stars in a timeless
        sky:
The light of a good man's life
        shines high,
Golden and splendid
Long after his brief earth years are
        ended.

GRACE V. WATKINS

I don't believe you dead. How can you be dead if I still
feel you? Maybe, like God, you changed into something
different that I'll have to speak to in a different way, but
you not dead to me Nettie. And never will be. Sometime
when I git tired of talking to myself I talk to you.

ALICE WALKER, *The Color Purple*

56

I know how alone you are
When it's so hard to be so far
From the ones who mean the most to you
When you would so much rather
  Have them close to you
I hope you know you haven't been forsaken
Goodbye don't mean I'm gone.

CAROLE KING

"*B*ut I don't understand. He is in heaven. He would be too happy to care for anything that is going on in this woeful world."

"Perhaps that is so," she said, smiling a sweet contradiction to her words, "but I don't believe it."

"What do you believe?"

"Many things that I have to say to you, but you cannot understand them now."

"I have sometimes wondered, for I cannot help it," I said, "whether he is shut off from all knowledge of me for all these years till I can go to him. It will be a great while. It seems hard. Roy would want to know something, if it were only a little, about me."

"I believe that he wants to know, and that he knows, Mary; though, since the belief must rest on analogy and conjecture, you need not accept it as demonstrated mathematics," she answered, with another smile.

"Roy never forgot me here!" I said, not meaning to sob.

"That's just it. He was not constituted so that he, remaining himself, Roy, could forget you. If he goes out into his other life forgetting, he becomes another than himself. . . . It seems to me to lie just here: Roy loved you. Our Father, for some tender, hidden reason, took him out of your sight for a while. Though changed much, he can have forgotten nothing. Being *only out of sight*, you remember, not lost, nor asleep, nor annihilated, he goes on loving. To love must mean to think of, to care for, to hope for, to pray for, not less out of body than in it."

ELIZABETH STUART PHELPS, *The Gates Ajar*

ELEGY FOR HERACLITUS

They told me, Heraclitus, they told me
        you were dead.
They brought me bitter news to hear
        and bitter tears to shed.
I wept as I remembered how often
        you and I
Had tired the sun with talking
        and sent him down the sky.
And now that thou art lying, my dear
        old Carian guest,
A handful of gray ashes,
        long, long ago at rest,
Still are thy pleasant voices,
        the nightingale awake:
For Death, he taketh all away,
        but these he cannot take.

by CALLIMACHUS, a Greek sculptor, about HERACLITUS, a
Greek philosopher, 3rd century B.C.

We give back, to you, Oh God, those whom you gave to
us. You did not lose them when you gave them to us, and
we do not lose them by their return to you. . . . Open our
eyes to see more clearly, and draw us closer to you that we
may know that we are nearer to our loved ones, who are
with you.

WILLIAM PENN

Where we love is home,
Home that our feet may leave,
but not our hearts.

OLIVER WENDELL HOLMES

DYING

The willow tree —
ancient symbol
of the house
of mourning

Rick refused to die. As cancer invaded his body, he experienced more pain than he had ever known in Vietnam. Yet, he pushed himself to move, talk, live. His goal was to get home to his wife and fourteen-month-old "miracle baby"—the baby he was told he never could have.

For three months I helped Rick fight. As my care for him grew, so did my torment. I wanted to tell him he would live and feed his hope. I wanted to tell him he would not live and help him die.

Suddenly Rick's own thoughts were more than he could bear. Unable to share his fear and depression, he became hostile to everyone around him. For two weeks he refused to see his family.

Another medical emergency brought death closer than ever to Rick. An entire day passed before I found the courage to enter his room. He was quite alert, yet still. When I sat down beside him, he said, "Jill, please lay your head on my shoulder. Just for a minute. Please." I did. . . . He cried.

We began a slow, painstaking conversation.

"How long are you going to live, Rick?"
"I don't know, Jill. I just don't know."
"Rick, what do you live for?"

"My wife. My baby. You know I live for my family, Jill."

"Then be with them, Rick."

"I hear you, Jill."

Within five minutes after I left, Rick's family arrived. Within one hour after I left, Rick died.

CHAPTER TWO is about fighting. We have been fighting death all our lives. As babies at birth we fought death as we gasped for air in order to live. And now, if we accept Chapter One's encouragement to celebrate the gift of life, how can we not battle against the taker of life? Chapter Two does not romanticize death. Instead, selections boldly confront the tragedy in all its ugliness.

Rick's struggle involved turning away those closest to him. Suffering induces many moods and behaviors, sometimes ones that are entirely foreign to us. Certain quotes in Chapter Two will help you understand your own actions. Others will help you understand those around you. You will not be informed of a *right* way to grieve. A struggle is a struggle. Chapter Two seeks only to relate to and demystify your experiences. Where there is clarity, there is comfort. Where there is understanding, there is withstanding.

Eventually Rick released his fears upon the shoulders of his loved ones. From Shakespeare to Buscaglia we are told to "give sorrow words." Poetry and prose that encourage verbal expression, often coupled with tears, abound throughout history. Furthermore, much contemporary literature stresses the need to "work through" or "deal with" a grievous situation. One intent of Chapter Two is to explain just what this process is. Though some comments may seem forceful or difficult to accept, do not be disheartened. Simply by reading *A Rumor of Angels* you are boldly dealing with your own struggle.

*T*he human mind is as little capable to contemplate death for any length of time as the eye is able to look at the sun.

LA ROCHEFOUCAULD

*A*s men are not able to fight against death, misery, ignorance, they have taken it into their heads, in order to be happy, not to think about it at all.

BLAISE PASCAL

*G*o, go, go, said the bird: human kind
Cannot bear very much reality.

T. S. ELIOT

*W*hen a person is born we rejoice, and when they're married we jubilate, but when they die we try to pretend nothing has happened.

MARGARET MEAD

*J*ust realize, I am 69 and I have never seen a person die. I have never even been in the same house while a person died. How about birth? An obstetrician invited me to see my first birth only last year. Just think, these are the greatest events of life and they have been taken out of our experience. We somehow hope to live full emotional lives when we have carefully expunged the sources of the deepest human emotions.

GEORGE WALD

*W*ho is the happy, successful American? Answer this question by looking at the advertising in popular magazines. Notice the emphasis on youthfulness, vitality, and productivity. The worth of a man is measured by what he can produce. Doing is the criterion for being. Little wonder that Americans have such difficulty handling leisure time or retirement! I have a friend who spends every vacation in a remote wilderness spot, chopping wood and pumping water, and every year he returns from his vacation exhausted but released from the guilt he felt about taking time off work. Vitality is the foundation of this lifestyle. We place a huge premium on the aggressive, vigorous individual filled with boundless energy. Little wonder that death, the direct opposite of vital life, is denied.

RICHARD W. DOSS

*D*eath is a quiet person and kind of scary. He does not say much but is very sharp and it is almost impossible to outsmart him. Although you would like to stay away from him, there's something about him that kind of draws you to him. You like him and fear him at the same time. I picture Death as being millions of years old but only looking about forty.

ANONYMOUS

I know that I shall die soon and my mind is reconciled to it; but when I think that my body will be put into a coffin, that the lid of the coffin will be screwed down and I will be buried under the earth, I am horrified. I am well aware that my horror is unreasonable, that I shall not be feeling anything by then, but I cannot overcome this feeling. Sometimes I also have the feeling—and that is also unreasonable—that I shall not die. I read somewhere that a Frenchman had begun his will with the words: "Not *when* but *if* I should die one day. . . ."

ALEXANDER SERGEYEVICH BUTURLIN

*"D*ying," he said to me, "is a very dull dreary affair." Suddenly he smiled. "And my advice to you is to have nothing whatever to do with it," he added.

SOMERSET MAUGHAM, shortly before his death in 1965, as recorded by his nephew, ROBIN MAUGHAM

*Y*et even our ties to earth-death are being systematically cut off. We neither kill nor harvest the food for our own tables. It comes to us already death-processed. We have no bone-deep knowledge that other things die so that we may eat and live. . . . Outside, the world itself dies every year. We have almost forgotten that. The sun withdraws its light, the darkness overshadows the earth. The waters freeze and the leaves decay. We forget because we don't have to live in that world anymore. We have created our own world where we have as much light and heat as we desire, hot running water, and fresh fruit the year round. We exempt ourselves from the season of death that envelops the world outside our artificial environment.

VIRGINIA STEM OWENS

Tarry awhile, O Death, I
    cannot die
With all my blossoming
    hopes unharvested,
My joys ungarnered, all my
    songs unsung,
And all my tears unshed.

Tarry awhile, till I am
    satisfied
Of love and grief, of earth
    and altering sky;
Till all my human hungers
    are fulfilled,
O Death, I cannot die!

SAROJINI NAIDU

When I realized that I was going to die, my first reaction
was not so much terror but affront. That this could happen
to me now, before I was ready, before I'd done the big
works I intended to do and was surely worthy of; that this
could happen unexpectedly and immediately to me, who
had to be present, of necessity, in order to notice, in order
to keep track, because, obviously, if I were not present I
could not keep track, and who, then, would? I had never
thought consciously of myself as important, but of course,
in common with all other humans, I felt that I was the
pivot, the point of view, of the world. And to think of life
continuing in its daily way without me there . . . was very
nearly incomprehensible.

AGNES DE MILLE

And does it not seem hard to you,
When all the sky is clear and blue,
And I should like so much to play,
To have to go to bed by day?

ROBERT LOUIS STEVENSON

*E*merging hopes and wishes
    Die like waves
    Leaving a shore
And only moments before
    They were
    Frothing and glistening

WILLIAM J. RICE

Death lies on
her like an
untimely frost
Upon the sweetest
flower of all
the field

—WILLIAM SHAKESPEARE

*D*eath is always and under all circumstances a tragedy, for if it is not, then it means that life itself has become one.

THEODORE ROOSEVELT

*D*idn't they realize that to die is to die, whether you are seventeen, forty-nine, or one hundred and ten? Didn't they know that our death is our death? And that each one of us has only one death to die? This was my father's death! It was no less significant because he was most of a hundred. It was his death. The only one he would ever have.

JOSEPH W. MATHEWS

For a long moment they sit still without moving. She stares at him as though she's trying to memorize him. He smiles down at her. The moment passes and she glances away. . . .

ETHEL

. . . Norman. (*A pause*) This was the first time I've really felt we're going to die.

NORMAN

I've known it all along.

ETHEL

Yes, I know. But when I looked at you across the room, I could really see you dead. I could see you in your blue suit and a white starched shirt, lying in Thomas's Funeral Parlor on Bradshaw Street, your hands folded on your stomach, a little smile on your face.

NORMAN

How did I look?

ETHEL

Not good, Norman.

NORMAN

Which tie was I wearing?

ETHEL

I don't know.

NORMAN

How about the one with the pictures of the man fishing? Did you pack that one?

ETHEL

Shut up, Norman. (*Pause*) You've been talking about dying ever since I met you. It's been your favorite topic of conversation. And I've *had* to think about it. Our parents, my sister and brother, your brother, their wives, our dearest friends, practically everyone from the old days on Golden Pond, all dead. I've seen death, and touched death, and feared it. But today was the first time I've *felt* it [italics added].

ERNEST THOMPSON, *On Golden Pond*

*O*ne of these days soon I've got to face Mr. Death. . . . it's a dreadful thing, if you stop to think about it, the most dreadful thing in the world.

DR. KARL MENNINGER

*M*y God! My God! . . . I'm dying. . . . it may happen this moment. There was light and now there is darkness. I was here and now I'm going there! . . . There will be nothing. . . . Can this be dying? No, I don't want to!

LEO TOLSTOY, *The Death of Ivan Ilych*

*A*nd He withdrew from them about a stone's throw, and He knelt down and began to pray, saying, "Father, if Thou art willing, remove this cup from Me; yet not My will, but Thine be done." Now an angel from heaven appeared to Him, strengthening Him. And being in agony He was praying very fervently, and His sweat became like drops of blood, falling down upon the ground.

LUKE 22:41–44

*T*he adventurous life is not one exempt from fear, but on the contrary, one that is lived in full knowledge of fears of all kinds, one in which we go forward in spite of our fears. Many people have the utopian idea that others are less afraid than they are, and they feel therefore that they are inferior. All men are afraid, even desperately afraid. . . . Fear is a part of human nature.

PAUL TOURNIER

72

*T*here is no shame in avoiding elephants.

VIETNAMESE PROVERB

I found out that no one is ever prepared for death and that grief has nothing to do with intelligence.

DR. ROBERTA TEMES

*H*e who pretends to look on death without fear lies. All men are afraid of dying, this is the great law of sentient beings, without which the entire human species would soon be destroyed.

JEAN-JACQUES ROUSSEAU

I'm not afraid to die. I just don't want to be there when it happens.

WOODY ALLEN

*W*hether or not we admit it to ourselves, we are all haunted by a truly awful sense of impermanence. I have always had a particularly keen sense of this at New York cocktail parties, and perhaps that is why I drink the martinis almost as fast as I can snatch them from the tray.

TENNESSEE WILLIAMS

*T*he attempt to ban death from our consciousness is not only unsuccessful, but also detrimental to the quality of our lives. Even if we succeed in repressing the content of our fears, the feelings attached to it will manifest themselves in the form of vague, free-floating anxiety. We can never get rid of the fear unless we know what it is that we are fearing.

LISL MARBURG GOODMAN

We ignore the outer darkness;
or if we cannot ignore it,
if it presses too insistently upon us,
we disapprove of being afraid.

ALDOUS HUXLEY

Many fears are born of fatigue and loneliness. Beyond a
wholesome discipline, be gentle with yourself.

MAX EHRMANN

We are so conditioned to "think positively" that many
people secretly believe that if they directly experience their
fear and acknowledge it to someone, they will collapse into
it and never get back out. Of course this is not true.

STEPHANIE MATTHEWS SIMONTON

What a silly world we live in, where we believe that
everything has to be on a high, joyous level all the
time. . . . We learn that from the media. We turn on our
television set and we see people giddy over cornflakes. . . .

LEO F. BUSCAGLIA

"People who get sick don't necessarily behave well. Certainly they don't even come close to the Hollywood ideal—Ali MacGraw going down the tubes without damaging her looks or her spunk. People who are sick get pugnacious, or uncooperative, or desperately cranky. They yell at their relatives, complain about their nurses, accuse their doctors of incompetence. And somehow, through it all, I think many of us who take care of sick people preserve this idea that they have some responsibility to behave in an exemplary style. . . . I remember a four-year-old boy who was dying; he screamed and carried on and attacked any doctor who came near him. So we asked a child psychiatrist to come by and see him, and the child psychiatrist reported back to us that he was terrified of dying." Pause. "Actually, that's quite appropriate under the circumstances," the psychiatrist told us, gently.

PERRI KLASS

Don't bother me, can't you see I am busy dying?

H. G. WELLS, last words

No one ever falls apart seriously in the ideal world of the TV commercial. Why? Because it's unpleasant to see someone in emotional pain. Emotional pain, unlike physical pain, is not acceptable in our culture. Unlike the seemingly acceptable violence of television, it makes the viewer feel responsible and guilty in some vague, discomforting way.
  Grief is taboo.

ALLA BOZARTH-CAMPBELL, PH.D.

*B*ut all my energies, then and later, were exerted in holding myself together. I always had this Humpty Dumpty fantasy that if I allowed myself to crack, no one, not "all the King's men" could ever put me back together again. I'm beginning to learn how wrong I was. Emotions can strengthen you, not splinter you. To express emotions is healthier than to repress them.

LYNN CAIN

*M*y heart is broken
It is worn out at the knees
Hearing muffled
Seeing blind
Soon it will hit the Deep
    Freeze

And something is cracking
I don't know where
Ice on the sidewalk
Brittle branches
In the air.

SUZANNE VEGA

*W*hile grief is fresh, every attempt to divert it only irritates.

SAMUEL JOHNSON

Of all the sad sights in the world
　　The downfall of an Autumn leaf
　　Is grievous and suggesteth grief:
Who thought when Spring was fresh unfurled
Of this? When Spring-twigs gleamed impearled
Who thought of frost that nips the world?

CHRISTINA ROSSETTI

The whole issue of pain, evil, and suffering is a difficult
one to deal with, especially in the midst of depression.
Because our griefstricken emotions often cloud and distort
reality, it is hard to acknowledge that no one can be
blamed for our loss. All our senses look for a scapegoat.
We want to give someone credit for our misery.

PAM W. VREDEVELT

I cannot forgive my friends for dying: I do not find these
vanishing acts of theirs at all amusing.

LOGAN PEARSALL SMITH

I want to seize fate by the throat.

LUDWIG VAN BEETHOVEN

*W*orking at the hospital one soon learned death is not
reserved for the aged, nor is it fair in the type of illness it
wishes on its victims. I don't believe I ever reached the
"Why me" stage. I saw too many without a reason why.

LOUISE, quoted by ELISABETH KÜBLER-ROSS

*W*e must not expect simple answers to far-reaching questions. However far our gaze penetrates, there are always heights which block our vision.

ALFRED NORTH WHITEHEAD

I stop in this moment of stillness, and I know deep inside that the battle is not mine to win. It's beyond me. It's very complicated. I realize most of all that you did not send this trouble. It is part of the evil in our imperfect world. O dear Lord, direct my energies as a parent, and don't let me crumble.

CHARLOTTE ADELSPERGER

*T*he hardest part of faith is the last half hour.

DAVID WILKERSON

*N*ow is my misery full, and namelessly
it fills me. I am stark, as the stone's
inside is stark.
Hard as I am, I know one thing:
You grew—
. . . and grew
in order to stand forth
as too great pain
quite beyond my heart's grasping.
Now you are lying straight across my lap,
now I can no longer
give you birth.

RAINER MARIA RILKE

*A*bsence infects the air
And it is everywhere.
How can I shake off woe,
On what bed lay me down without you?

What healing sacrament
What ritual invent
And quietly perform
To bring life back and make it warm?

Another day a letter
Might tell you I am better,
The invalid has taken
Some food, is less forlorn and shaken.

But for today it's true
That I can hardly draw
A solitary breath
That does not hurt me like a little death.

MAY SARTON, *Halfway To Silence*

*H*e touched his heart but it did not beat, nor did he lift his eyes again. When Gilgamesh touched his heart it did not beat. So Gilgamesh laid a veil, as one veils the bride, over his friend. He began to rage like a lion, like a lioness robbed of her whelps. This way and that he paced round the bed, he tore out his hair and strewed it around. He dragged off his splendid robes and flung them down as though they were abominations. . . . Gilgamesh lamented; seven days and seven nights he wept for Enkidu, until the worm fastened on him. Only then he gave him up to the earth. . . .

EPIC OF GILGAMESH, story of the third millennium B.C.

Take pity on me, O Lord,
　　I am in trouble now.
Grief wastes away my eye,
　　My throat, my inmost parts.

For my life is worn out with sorrow,
　　my years with sighs;
My strength yields under misery,
　　my bones are wasting away.
I am contemptible,
　　Loathsome to my neighbours,
to my friends a thing of fear.

PSALM 31:9–11

God strengthen me to bear myself,
That heaviest weight of all to bear,
Inalienable weight of care.

CHRISTINA ROSSETTI

Weary am I of my heart's bereavements, and too old to put forth branches anew. One by one I have lost my friends and foes, and the path of melancholy pleasures that lies before me is all too clear. . . . Laden am I with useless treasure, as with music that has lost its potency for ever. Reveal Thyself to me, O Lord; for all things are hard to one who has lost touch with God.

ANTOINE DE SAINT-EXUPÉRY, *The Wisdom of the Sands*

I was just as crazy as you can be and still be at large. I didn't have any really normal minutes during those two years. It wasn't just grief. It was total confusion. I was nutty. . . .

HELEN HAYES, quoted by LYNN CAIN

*M*y doctor was like a priest to me during times when I felt guilty in a period of mourning. "If you had been able to act differently then, you would have acted differently," she would say. It took me a long time to realize that it is simply not in our power to play out our lives in perfect ways.

ANN KAISER STEARNS, *Living Through Personal Crisis*

*L*ord. . . .
Please recognize our panic as a prayer.

KIT KUPERSTOCK

*N*o one ever told me that grief felt so like fear. I am not afraid, but the sensation is like being afraid. The same fluttering in the stomach, the same restlessness, the yawning. I keep on swallowing.

C. S. LEWIS

*G*rief is as varied as fish in the river,
Sometimes small and visible in shallows,
Sometimes large and mired in the bottom,
and everything in between.

NEAL BOWERS

*B*elieve me, every man has his secret sorrows, which the
world knows not; and oftentimes we call a man cold when
he is only sad.

HENRY WADSWORTH LONGFELLOW

*S*ometimes, Davie, laughter is a kind of crying when
grieving has left you exhausted and your tears are spent.
We just stood in the hallway holding each other and
laughing. . . . We felt too bad to risk our tears again.

MARIE ROTHENBERG and MEL WHITE, *David*

*H*e disliked emotion, not because he felt lightly, but
because he felt deeply.

JOHN BUCHAN

*W*e must not assume that a person is not suffering intense
sorrow simply because he is not showing it. Instead, we
must develop a feeling of empathy for that person so that
we can truly say we are sorry for him in his loss.

JANE BURGESS KOHN

Though I kept a space of privacy between me and others, I hungered for the intimate, tender support system so easily available to the children. A widower needs a wholly receiving audience for his endless ramblings of fear and sorrow. As much as a child he needs physical contact to comfort his tears and counteract his aloneness. The subtraction of his wife alters his identity, and he needs his self-esteem restored. He needs to sense an escape route out of anxiety and pain. He needs somebody entirely focused on him. The bereaved who have such a person do recover faster.

RICHARD MERYMAN

Sorrow is like a precious treasure, shown only to friends.

AFRICAN PROVERB

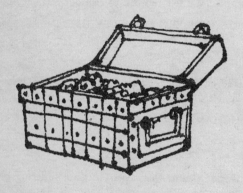

I knew. He knew. He knew that I knew. I knew that he knew that I knew. . . . The knowledge was too wounding, too burning, too enormously devastating to touch with words or even looks.

LYNN CAIN

The deeper the sorrow the less tongue it hath.

THE TALMUD

I sometimes hold it half a sin
        To put in words the grief I feel;
        For words, like Nature, half reveal
And half conceal the Soul within.

But, for the unquiet heart and brain,
        A use in measured language lies;
        The sad mechanic exercise,
Like dull narcotics, numbing pain.

In words, like weeds, I'll wrap me o'er,
        Like coarsest clothes against the cold;
        But that large grief which these enfold
Is given in outline and no more.

ALFRED, LORD TENNYSON

*I*t is such a secret place, the land of tears.

ANTOINE DE SAINT-EXUPÉRY

I could lie down like a tired child,
And weep away the life of care
Which I have borne and yet must bear,
Till death like sleep might shed on me.

PERCY BYSSHE SHELLEY

Sorrow makes us all children again.

RALPH WALDO EMERSON

The thistle—
symbol of
earthly sorrow

Go ahead and let yourself cry. Let somebody hold and support you. When you do, you'll find that a lot of your tiredness and lack of energy will start to lift.

STEPHANIE MATTHEWS SIMONTON

The sorrow which has no vent in tears may make other organs weep.

HENRY MAUDSLEY

He said, "You have to tell such people to lay off cliches about boys not crying. I told my kids, 'It's rough on us losing Mother; it really hurts a lot.' I cry with my children and tell my eighteen-year-old son that it takes a man to cry."

WILLARD K. KOHN

*F*rom a physiological view, when there is emotional stress, gastric secretion increases. Crying not only helps relieve tension but aids in the excretion of lysozyme, which reduces the concentration of gastric juices. A result is a lower incidence of duodenal ulcers in females (six to eight times less frequent in females than in males). . . . You do not need statistics or clinical cases to demonstrate a truth known to many of us: whatever your age or sex, you simply feel better after a good cry.

EARL A. GROLLMAN

*H*uman beings ritualize events in order to limit realities that are too much to bear—to contain them in formal patterns to make them bearable . . .

Funerals are the rituals we create to help us face the reality of death, to give us a way of expressing our response to that reality with other persons, and to protect us from the full impact of the meaning of death for ourselves . . . One funeral I attended was full of the music that the dead person had loved in life. In perfect counterpoint to the music came the rhythms of his loving aunt's sobbing, the outpouring of her heart in the midst of family and friends who could share her sorrow. It was perfectly appropriate to the reality of life and loss . . .

ALLA BOZARTH-CAMPBELL, PH.D.

*I*n regard to these kinds of losses, nothing hurts more than not being given the opportunities to express pent-up feelings and emotions, not being able to submit to the pain . . . Nothing hurts more than the deep fear that deceased sons and daughters are being forgotten because no one ever talks of them again.

RONALD J. KNAPP

Give sorrow words; the grief that does not speak
Whispers the oe'r fraught heart, and bids it break.

WILLIAM SHAKESPEARE, *Macbeth*

*F*rom then on I lived at Viareggio, finding courage from
the radiance of Eleanora's eyes. She used to rock me in her
arms, consoling my pain, but not only consoling, for she
seemed to take my sorrow to her own breast, and I
realized that if I had not been able to bear the society of
other people, it was because they all played the comedy of
trying to cheer me with forgetfulness. Whereas Eleanora
said:

"Tell me about Dierdre and Patrick," and made me
repeat to her all their little sayings and ways, and show her
their photos, which she kissed and cried over. She never
said, "Cease to grieve," but she grieved with me, and, for
the first time since their death, I felt I was not alone.

ISADORA DUNCAN

SONNET ON CATHERINE WORDSWORTH

Surprised by joy—impatient as the Wind
I turned to share the transport—O! with whom
But thee, deep buried in the silent tomb,
That spot which no vicissitude can find?
Love, faithful love, recalled thee to my mind—
But how could I forget thee? Through what power,
Even for the least division of an hour,
Have I been so beguiled as to be blind
To my most grievous loss? That thought's return
Was the worst pang that sorrow ever bore,
Save one, one only, when I stood forlorn,
Knowing my heart's best treasure was no more;
That neither present time, nor years unborn
Could to my sight that heavenly face restore.

WILLIAM WORDSWORTH

Sadness, as actually existing, causes pleasure, since it brings
to mind that which is loved, the absence of which causes
sadness; and yet the mere thought of it gives pleasure.

ST. THOMAS AQUINAS

Four ducks on a pond,
A grass-bank beyond,
A blue sky of spring,
White clouds on the wing:
What a little thing
to remember for years—
To remember with tears!

WILLIAM ALLINGHAM

Grief fills the room up of my absent child,
Lies in his bed, walks up and down with me,
Puts on his pretty looks, repeats his words,
Remembers me of all his gracious parts,
Stuffs out his vacant garments with his form:
Then have a reason to be fond of grief.

WILLIAM SHAKESPEARE, *King John*

The death of any familiar person—the death, even, of a
dog or cat—whether loved or not leaves an emptiness. The
great tree goes down and leaves an empty place against the
sky. If the person is deeply loved and deeply familiar the
void seems greater than all the world remaining. . . . But
grief is a form of love—the longing for the dear face, the
warm hand. It is the remembered reality of the beloved
that calls it forth. For an instant she is *there*, and the void
denied.

SHELDON VANAUKEN

Grief carries its own anesthesia. It gets you over a lot.

MRS. LYNDON JOHNSON, after the death of her husband

Mourning. . . . You seem to be filled with it. Always. In a sense, like a pregnancy. But . . . pregnancy imparts a sense of doing something even while inactive, [whereas] mourning bequeaths a sense of futility and meaninglessness in the midst of activity. . . . My everydayness has snapped and I am in quarantine from the world. Want nothing from it, have nothing to give to it. When things get too bad, the whole world is lost to you, the world and the people in it. . . .

. . . .

Some days I can look at her photograph and the image revives me, reinforces her for me. On other days, I gaze at her and am blinded with tears. Newly bereft. . . .

TOBY TALBOT

Grief is like a long and winding valley where any bend may reveal a totally new landscape . . . Sometimes the surprise is the opposite one; you are presented with exactly the same sort of country you thought you left behind miles ago. That is when you wonder whether the valley isn't a circular trench. But it isn't. There are partial recurrences but the sequence doesn't repeat.

C. S. LEWIS

Sometimes in life, our spirits are nearly gone . . .
sometimes we feel so crushed and broken and
        overwhelmed . . .
that we do not even see where we are going.
We are just out there walking to keep the
        heart beating . . .
        and the circulation moving.
but . . . if that is all we can do . . .
        and we are doing it . . .
that is still being faithful . . . not quitting . . .
        giving it our best.

ann kiemel

We survivors, we who are left behind, know the
frustration of helplessness. We carry on because it does not
help if we don't. We function, not out of strength, but in
the absence of any alternative.

. . . .

I found my mood determined by the direction of the wind
or the colors of the sky. Emotions associated with names
and places emerged. Emotions, long buried, emotions that
time could not touch, nor life sustain. My dreams and
recollections blended, and one became no more real than
the other.

My habits, so familiar, remained unchanged. . . .
Nothing in the world had changed to mark this
devastating loss in my life.

And in my need to carry on I lost myself in the daily
habits and occurrences of living.

SAMANTHA MOONEY

I had not known that the body bore so much,
That so bereaved it still would walk and thrive:
I had not known that, with no sense of touch,
An individual could stay alive.

WITTER BYNNER

*H*ere I stand. I can do no other. God help me. Amen.

MARTIN LUTHER

I sit here in this big house by myself trying to sew, but
what good is sewing gon do? What good is anything?
Being alive begin to seem like a awful strain.

ALICE WALKER, *The Color Purple*

*I*n times like these of such intense physical pain, confusion
and doubt, one must simply decide and do, decide and
do—and laugh a bit amidst the consequences.

TIM HANSEL, *You Gotta Keep Dancin'*

LAMENT

Listen, children:
Your father is dead:
From his old
   coats
I'll make you little jackets;
I'll make you little trousers
From his old pants.
There'll be in his pockets
Things he used to put
   there,
Keys and pennies
Covered with tobacco;
Dan shall have the pennies
To save in his bank;
Anne shall have the keys
To make a pretty noise
   with.
Life must go on.
And the dead be forgotten;
Life must go on,
Though good men die;
Anne, eat your
   breakfast;
Dan, take your medicine;
Life must go on;
I forget just why.

EDNA ST. VINCENT MILLAY

One aspect of deep grief is loss of the imagination. One cannot imagine a time when one is not in pain.

.   .   .   .

How many times have I sabotaged myself by leaping ahead of my own healing process, trying so desperately to "feel better" that I make myself feel even worse because I have added to my primary pain the new complication of failure! In cheating myself of the necessary time to feel bad I have cheated myself of the only process that could really heal me.

Ultimately, the only way to get through something is to get *through* it—not over, under, or around it, but all the way through it. And it takes as long as it takes.

ALLA BOZARTH-CAMPBELL, PH.D

*P*enny said, "You've seed how things goes in the world o' men. You've knowed men to be low-down and mean. You've seed ol' Death at his tricks. You've messed around with ol' Starvation. Ever' man wants life to be a fine thing, and easy. 'Tis fine, boy, powerful fine, but 'tain't easy. Life knocks a man down and he gits up and it knocks him down agin. I've been uneasy all my life."

MARJORIE KINNAN RAWLINGS, *The Yearling*

I've developed a new philosophy—I only dread one day at a time.

CHARLES M. SCHULZ, *Peanuts*

*L*ead, kindly Light, amid th'encircling gloom,
  Lead Thou me on;
The night is dark, and I am far from home;
  Lead Thou me on;
Keep Thou my feet; I do not ask to see
The distant scene—one step enough for me.

JOHN HENRY NEUMAN

Life is an onion and one peels it crying.

—FRENCH PROVERB

*F*ar from disassociating himself from our pain, the God of love, peace, hope and joy meets us right there at the very point of our hurt. . . . he calls us to face our own pain; he calls us to face the reality of our own unhappiness; he calls us to enter into our own suffering and to embrace the pain of others because it is there that we meet the one who has embraced the agony of the whole world in his death on the cross.

THE REV. KENNETH B. SWANSON, PH.D.

*A*nd I was having to bear the unbearable. If I must bear it, I *would* bear it—find the whole meaning of it, taste the whole of it. . . . I would *not* run away from grief; I would *not* try to hold on to it when—if, unbelievably—it passed.

SHELDON VANAUKEN

*D*earest friend, please believe that I understand the pain in your heart, the void in your gut, the cut-off feeling, the many things you never told her and the pain of knowing you never will. The agony of death, at this moment, for you is unbearable, but please, be patient. Time will soothe your pain.

With love and deep hope that the time will pass quickly for you. . . .

TERI, quoted by DR. ROBERTA TEMES

SMALL PRAYER

*C*hange, move, dead clock, that this fresh day
May break with dazzling light to these sick eyes.
Burn, glare, old sun, so long unseen,
That time may find its sand again, and cleanse
Whatever it is that a wound remembers
After the healing ends.

WELDON KEES

*I*n three words I can sum up everything I've learned about life. It goes on.

ROBERT FROST

*M*ost people though, manage to make their way through the painful stages of grief and eventually regain their emotional balance. What they need desperately are caring friends and relatives who allow them to grieve in their own way, at their own pace and who, above all, will not insist that they act like their "old selves." For no one who has suffered a terrible loss will ever be her old self again. She may be a different self or even a better self, but she will never regain the identity that was untouched by grief.

SUSAN JACOBY

*A*lthough we know that after such a loss the acute state of mourning will subside, we also know that we shall remain inconsolable and will never find a substitute. No matter what may fill the gap, even if it be filled completely, it nevertheless remains something else.

SIGMUND FREUD, letter he wrote on the day that his daughter, Sophie, would have been 36 years old

When grief and shock surpass endurance there occur phases of exhaustion of anesthesia in which relatively little is left and one has the illusion of recognizing, and understanding, a good deal. Throughout these days Mary had, during these breathing spells, drawn a kind of solace from the recurrent thought: at least I am enduring it. I am aware of what has happened, I am meeting it face to face, I am living through it. There had been, even, a kind of pride, a desolate kind of pleasure, in the feeling: I am carrying a heavier weight than I could have dreamed it possible for a human being to carry, yet I am living through it. It had of course occurred to her that this happens to many people, that it is very common, and she humbled and comforted herself in this thought.

JAMES AGEE

All the loves that we love are part of the same love.
All the deaths that we live through are part of
	the same dying.
And while we laugh or cry for different reasons,
The sound of happiness is much the same everywhere.
And tears, wept for whatever reason,
Always taste of salt.

MARILEE ZDENEK

*O*f course we're going to die . . . Doesn't everybody know that? And is that still something that is frightening? Of course, of course . . . For a person like myself, who has suffered serious ill health, it becomes part of your tissue; you think about it all the time. I don't say it's easy, and I don't mean to sound fatuous about it, but it doesn't make me unhappy. *Life* things make me unhappy, like getting through a day in New York.

Quote by MAURICE SENDAK from the article "Of Wild Things, Kids and Death" by *San Francisco Examiner* writer CAROLINE DREWES

*H*elp me to realize that I am not the only person who finds it difficult to start the day.

F. TOPPING

*N*o man is an island, entire of itself; every man is a piece of the continent, a part of the main; if a clod be washed away by the sea, Europe is the less, as well as if a promontory were, as well as if manor of thy friends or of thine own were; any man's death diminishes me, because I am involved in mankind; and therefore never send to know for whom the bell tolls; it tolls for thee.

JOHN DONNE

One of the things I find most astounding is that, though we think of the future life as something perfected, when Christ appeared to his disciples He said, "Come look at my hands," and He invited Thomas to put his finger into the print of the nail. Why did He want to keep the wounds of His humanity? Wasn't it because He wanted to carry back with Him an eternal reminder of the sufferings of those on earth? He carried the marks of suffering so He could continue to understand the needs of those suffering. He wanted to be forever one with us.

DR. PAUL BRAND, hand surgeon

Not a day passes over the earth, but men and women of no note do great deeds, speak great words and suffer noble sorrows.

CHARLES READE

Here is to the world that goes round on wheels.
Death is a thing that all man feels.
If living was a thing that money could buy,
The rich would live and the poor would die.

ANONYMOUS

*D*on't you remember sweet Alice, Ben Bolt—
    Sweet Alice whose hair was so brown,
Who wept with delight when you gave her a smile,
    And trembled with fear at your frown?

In the old churchyard in the valley, Ben Bolt,
    In a corner obscure and alone,
They have fitted a slab of the granite so gray
    And Alice lies under the stone.

And don't you remember the school, Ben Bolt,
    With the master so cruel and grim,
And the shaded nook in the running brook
    Where the children went to swim?

Grass grows on the master's grave, Ben Bolt,
    The spring of the brook is dry.
And of all the boys who were schoolmates then
    There are only you and I.

THOMAS DUNN ENGLISH

*I*n the spring of 1970, within six shocking weeks, my
good friend's teen-age daughter died of an embolism, my
husband's best friend died of cancer at age thirty-nine and
my mother's heart failed just short of her sixty-third
birthday. I lost my fear of flying that spring—I'll fly on
anything now—for I had become reacquainted with
mortality and I recognized that even if I stayed grounded
all of my life I still would die.

JUDITH VIORST

*T*here is an appointed time for everything.
And there is a time for every event under heaven—
A time to give birth, and a time to die. . . .
A time to weep, and a time to laugh;
A time to mourn, and a time to dance.

. . . .

No man has authority to restrain the wind with the wind,
nor authority over the day of death. . . .

ECCLESIASTES 3:1,2,4; 8:8

*D*eath is clearly no failure.

BARBARA GENEST

*N*umberless are the world's wonders, but none
More wonderful than man . . .
. . . from every wind
He has made himself secure—from all but one:
In the late wind of death he cannot stand.

SOPHOCLES

Death knocks,
as we know,
at the door
of the cottage
and of the
castle.

—ZULEIKA DOBSON

The man can neither make, nor retain, one moment of time; it all comes to him by pure gift; he might as well regard the sun and moon as his chattels.

C. S. LEWIS

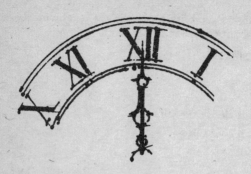

If none can 'scape death's dreadful dart,
    If rich and poor his beck obey,
If strong, if wise, if all do smart,
        Then I to 'scape shall have no way.
            Oh! grant me grace, O God, that I
            My life may mend, sith I must die.

ROBERT SOUTHWELL

We have finished our years like a sigh. . . .
So teach us to number our days,
That we may present to Thee a heart of wisdom.

PSALM 90:9,12

LETTING GO

Behold, I tell you a mystery — the trumpet will sound, and the dead will be raised imperishable.

*I*t was my last day of work and Rita's last week of life. For two months, since my new job offer, I had prepared myself to leave this hospital. For three months, since her diagnosis, Rita had prepared herself to leave this life.

I studied her face to find the words for good-bye. She had become one of those graced individuals who acquire a certain calmness and wisdom as death becomes a more present reality. I think I needed her blessing more than she needed mine.

"Jill," Rita said with a voice that seemed both young and old, "I wanted to give you a good-bye present but couldn't find anyone to go out and buy it. Please open my top drawer and take out ten dollars."

"Oh, Rita, I don't need your money to know that you appreciate and care about me."

Rita became stern. "Please, Jill. Take the money and buy a new pair of socks for yourself and think of me when you wear them."

I love my new socks.

CHAPTER THREE is about saying good-bye. Good-bye to life and good-bye to each other. But how does one get such a sweet spirit of acceptance that lets go and kisses good-bye? Chapter Three seeks to explain this mystery of peace that comes after torment; strength that comes after struggle; and wisdom that comes after confusion. C. S. Lewis, Isak Dinesen, Annie Dillard, and many others offer you glimpses into the hope and meaning they have found. As you read their thoughts, you will be challenged and inspired to open your own mind and heart to find for yourself the peace that surpasses understanding . . . and enables you to let go.

*T*hings have fallen apart, haven't they; that realization must come to all of us, it is a prerequisite to remedy.

GEORGE JACKSON, Soledad Prisoner

*I*n his last exhausting fight for life, only a few hours before he went to heaven, he declared, "Something good has got to come out of this."

CHARLOTTE ADELSPERGER

*Pure water lily
how grew you
so white
Rising through
dark water?*

—ADA C. PERRY

I am a more sensitive person, a more effective pastor, a more sympathetic counselor because of Aaron's life and death than I would ever have been without it. And I would give up all of those gains in a second if I could have my son back. If I could choose, I would forego all the spiritual growth and depth which has come my way because of our experiences, and be what I was fifteen years ago, an average rabbi, an indifferent counselor, helping some people and unable to help others, and the father of a bright, happy boy. But I cannot choose.

RABBI HAROLD KUSHNER, referring to the death of his firstborn

*T*he world breaks everyone, and afterward many are strong at the broken places.

ERNEST HEMINGWAY, *A Farewell to Arms*

I saw a very real change take place in Rico, particularly during the last six months when it became apparent to him that he was fighting a losing battle. It was like a calmness enveloped him. He wasn't what you would call moody, but more contemplative. He seemed to set aside boyish things and boyish behavior. . . . I think he displayed more control and wisdom during those last six months than most people do in a lifetime. He became my main support during that time.

RONALD J. KNAPP, quoting a mother whose 12-year-old son died of Ewing's tumor

*T*here is no birth of consciousness without pain.

CARL G. JUNG

*I*t is good for thee to dwell deep, that thou mayest feel and understand the spirits of people.

JOHN WOOLMAN

I do not believe that sheer suffering teaches. If suffering alone taught, all the world would be wise, since everyone suffers. To suffering must be added mourning, understanding, patience, love, openness and willingness to remain vulnerable.

ANNE MORROW LINDBERGH

*W*e must kick the darkness 'til it bleeds daylight.

BRUCE COCHBURN

*T*he self must be destroyed, brought down to nothing, in order for self-transcendence to begin. Then the self can begin to relate to powers beyond itself. It has to thrash around in its finitude, it has to "die," in order to question that finitude, in order to see beyond it.

ERNEST BECKER

The heart of the wise is in the house of the mourning.

—ECCLESIATES 7:14

*T*he single saying of Jesus which the Bible records more often than any other (four times) expresses a paradoxical truth: "Whoever finds his life will lose it, and whoever loses his life for my sake will find it." Sometimes seeming tragedies, like pain and suffering, can nudge us along the path to "losing our lives . . ."

PHILIP YANCEY

Self-surrender . . . takes away fear of death because you have already died, you have died to you as the center of you.

CURTIS JONES

"How does one become a butterfly?" she asked pensively.

"You must want to fly so much that you are willing to give up being a caterpillar."

"You mean to *die*?" asked Yellow. . . .

"Yes and No," he answered. "What *looks* like you will die But what's *really* you will still live."

TRINA PAULUS, *Hope for the Flowers*

The caterpillar—symbol of life on earth; the chrysalis-death; the butterfly—symbol of the resurrected life.

O Lord, by all thy dealings with us, whether of joy or pain, of light or darkness, let us be brought to thee. Let us value no treatment of thy grace simply because it makes us happy or because it makes us sad, because it gives us or denies us what we want; but may all that thou sendest us bring us to thee, knowing thy perfectness, we may be sure in every disappointment that thou art still loving us, and in every darkness that thou art still enlightening us, and in every enforced idleness that thou art still using us; yea, in every death thou art still giving us life, as in his death thou didst give life to thy Son, our Saviour, Jesus Christ. Amen.

PHILLIPS BROOKS

*P*ain casts us out of ourselves to seek healing and comfort from our friends and family and, at our deepest psychic and spiritual levels, pain casts us outside of ourselves to seek comfort and healing of God.

THE REV. KENNETH B. SWANSON, PH.D.

*T*he Lord is near to the brokenhearted, And saves those who are crushed in spirit.

PSALM 34:18

I have no wit, no words, no tears;
    My heart within me like a stone
Is numbed too much for hopes or fears.
    Look right, look left, I dwell alone;
I lift mine eyes, but dimmed with grief
    No everlasting hills I see;
My life is in the falling leaf:
    O Jesus, quicken me!

My life is like a faded leaf,
    My harvest dwindled to a husk;
Truly my life is void and brief
    And tedious in the barren dusk;
My life is like a frozen thing,
    No bud nor greenness can I see:
Yet rise it shall,—the sap of Spring;
    O Jesus, rise in me!

CHRISTINA ROSSETTI

*L*ife begins on the other side of despair.

JEAN-PAUL SARTRE

The second before the sun went out we saw a wall of dark shadow come speeding at us. We no sooner saw it than it was upon us, like thunder. It roared up the valley. It slammed our hill and knocked us out. It was the monstrous swift shadow cone of the moon. I have since read that this wave of shadow moves 1,800 miles an hour. Language can give no sense of this sort of speed—1,800 miles an hour. It was 195 miles wide. No end was in sight—you saw only the edge. It rolled at you across the land at 1,800 miles an hour, hauling darkness like plague behind it. . . .

Less than two minutes later, when the sun emerged, the trailing edge of the shadow cone sped away. It coursed down our hill and raced eastward over the plain and dropped over the planet's rim in a twinkling. It had clobbered us, and now it roared away. We blinked in the light.

ANNIE DILLARD, observations on the total eclipse at Yakima, Washington

The winter of the soul, in its seeming barrenness, its times of seeming unproductivity, its times of silence and seeming stalemate, is perhaps its most important season. Without it, there is no recovery of freshness and vitality; no bursting forth in springtime splendor.

DWIGHT H. JUDY

The lily
of the valley—
symbol of hope,
even in the
valley of despair.

The trumpet of a prophecy! O Wind,
If winter comes, can spring be far behind?

PERCY BYSSHE SHELLEY

116

*W*e see death all around us. Plants, animals, friends, family all die. We know, too, that we will die; but as we witness the glorious rebirth of nature in springtime, we inevitably ask ourselves, is death the ultimate and final end; does it have the last word to say about our life? . . . We may rationally reject the hope and confidence at the core of our being; it may well be a deception, the last trick, the ultimate deception of a vindictive, cruel and arbitrary universe. But the decisive religious question, perhaps the only religious question that really matters, is whether that hope which is at the center of our personality is cruel deception or whether it is a hint of an explanation, a rumor of angels, the best insight we have into what human life is all about.

ANDREW GREELEY

*T*he loftiest hope is the surest of being fulfilled.

GEORGE MACDONALD, *The Castle: A Parable*

*I*t is plain that the hope of a future life arises from the feeling, which exists in the breast of every man, that the temporal is inadequate to meet and satisfy the demands of his nature.

IMMANUEL KANT

I do not recall the time when
I was not conscious of a hunger
    for something
beyond the physical and the
material.

MARY SUE TYNES LUNDY

*M*y question, the question that had brought me to the edge of suicide when I was fifty years old, was the simplest question lying in the soul of every human being, from a silly child to the wisest of the elders, the question without which life is impossible; such was the way I felt about the matter. The question is this: What will come of what I do today and tomorrow? What will come of my entire life?

Expressed differently, the question may be: Why should I live? Why should I wish for anything or do anything? Or to put it still differently: Is there any meaning in my life that will not be destroyed by my inevitably approaching death?

. . . .

No matter what answers a given faith might provide for us, every answer of faith gives infinite meaning to the finite existence of man, meaning that is not destroyed by suffering, deprivation, and death. Therefore, the meaning of life and the possibility of living may be found in faith alone . . . faith is to answer the questions of a tsar dying in the midst of luxury, an old slave tormented in his labor; an ignorant child, an aged sage, a half-witted old lady, a happy young woman, and a youth consumed by passions . . .

LEO TOLSTOY

*S*eek not to understand that thou mayest believe, but believe that thou mayest understand.

ST. AUGUSTINE

I don't know who—or what—put the question, I don't know when it was put. I don't remember answering. But at some moment I did answer Yes to Someone—or Something—and from that hour I was certain that existence is meaningful and that, therefore, my life, in self-surrender, had a goal.

DAG HAMMARSKJÖLD

If it is true that there is Someone in charge of the whole mystery of life and death, we can hardly expect to escape a sense of futility and frustration until we begin to see what He is like and what His purposes are.

J. B. PHILLIPS

We shall not cease from exploration and the end of all our exploring will be to arrive where we started and know the place for the first time.

T. S. ELIOT

Long ago, I asked my parents
    (using other words)
      "Am I of value? Does my life have meaning?"
Then I asked my teachers,
    later, directors and editors,
    husband and friends—
      "Am I of value? Does my life have meaning?"
Then I asked God and God said, "Yes."

MARILEE ZDENEK

*F*or myself, I find some measure of reassurance against the nagging doubt of meaninglessness in the implications of what has been considered by some thinkers as the profoundest, even though unanswerable, question: Why is there something rather than nothing? What this question implies is that there is no necessity of there being a world at all. But precisely because it would have been so easy not to have been, the existence of the world and of my own individual self must have a significance, a meaning that goes beyond the mere fact of its and my own existing.

JACQUES CHORON

O Lord, Thou hast searched me and known me. . . .
For Thou didst form my inward parts:
Thou didst weave me in my mother's womb.
I will give thanks to Thee, for I am fearfully
    and wonderfully made. . . .
And in Thy book they were all written,
The days that were ordained for me,
When as yet there was not one of them.

PSALM 139:1,13–14–16

I looked down the valley of Granite Creek. . . . The whole course of the stream was visible, from the tickling snowpack through lush forest to the burning plain where it gave up its ghosts. I saw that stream in all phases of its life—as God might see in my life or my country's life—under the aspect of eternity. No trout could have such a view, and I tried to imagine them asking, in some flickering, troutlike way, where their creek began or whether it reached the sea.

JOHN TALLMADGE

*A*t any given moment, life is completely senseless. But viewed over a period, it seems to reveal itself as an organism existing in time, having a purpose, tending in a certain direction.

ALDOUS HUXLEY

My life has been a tapestry between my God and me;
I do not choose the colors, He worketh steadily.
Oftimes He weaveth sorrow, And I, in foolish pride,
Forget He sees the upper and I the underside.
But the dark threads, they're as needful
In the Skillful Weaver's hand
As the threads of gold and silver
In the pattern He has planned.

ANONYMOUS

We would be saved from all kinds of mistakes if we
always looked at things in the light of eternity.

WILLIAM BARCLAY

That is what mortals misunderstand. They say of some
temporal suffering, "No future bliss can make up for it,"
not knowing that Heaven, once attained, will work
backwards and turn even the agony into a glory.

C. S. LEWIS, *The Great Divorce*

Life must be understood backwards.

SÖREN KIERKEGAARD

*F*or I consider that the sufferings of this present time are not worthy to be compared with the glory that is to be revealed to us. . . .

. . . .

Now we see but a poor reflection as in a mirror; then we shall see face to face. Now I know in part; then I shall know fully, even as I am fully known.

ROMANS 8:18, I CORINTHIANS 13:12–13

*F*aith is to believe what we do not see, and the reward of this faith is to see what we believe.

ST. AUGUSTINE

*A*nd I was wondering if you had been to the mountain to look at the valley below? Did you see all the roads tangled down in the valley? Did you know which way to go? Oh the mountain stream runs pure and clear and I wish to my soul I could always be here. But there's a reason for living way down in the valley that only the mountain knows.

NOEL PAUL STOOKEY

*N*either despise nor oppose what thou dost not understand.

WILLIAM PENN

FARTHER ALONG

Tempted and tried, we're oft made to wonder
Why it should be thus all the day long.
While there are others living above us;
Never molested, though in the wrong.

Farther along we'll know all about it;
Farther along we'll understand why.
Cheer up my brothers, live in the sunshine,
We'll understand it all by and by.

SOUTHERN GOSPEL HYMN

And whether or not it is clear to you, no doubt the
universe is unfolding as it should. Therefore be at peace
with God. . . .

MAX EHRMANN

Indeed, I am persuaded that there is nothing in the arsenal
of medical or psychological technology that equals the
power inherent in a simple faith.

ROBERT VENINGA

Having faith is a necesary step toward one of two things.
Being healed is one of them. Peace of mind, if healing
doesn't come, is the other. Either one will suffice.

BRIAN STERNBERG, paralyzed from the neck down due to a
trampoline accident

*W*hen praying for healing, ask great things of God and expect great things from God. But let us seek for that healing that really matters, the healing of the heart. . . .

ARLO F. NEWELL

*I*t is more important, more thrilling, more satisfying and infinitely more valuable to know the Healer than to be healed.

ANONYMOUS

I noted that the faces of people who have a terminal disease, and who have come to terms with their own impending death, have a look that is a marvelous combination of tranquility and incredible power and insight.

MAL WARSHAW

"You're going to die," I said to myself. "This is really it and you had better say something definitive, something that will sum up your life."

The necessity to pronounce harassed me because, quite frankly, I could think of nothing to say. And I fretted through the long hours until it occurred to me, in the middle of the night, that I really didn't need to say anything at all. Nobody expected it or even wanted it. Having talked all my life ceaselessly, it seemed likely that if I hadn't said what I'd meant to say by now, it wasn't from lack of trying, and that, in fact, my whole life was what I had to say; my habits of living were my statements. . . .

. . . .

What else did I dare think about? Not so very much. Nothing profound. I didn't kick against fate. The fact was, I had had a long and vigorous life. While I had had my body I had used it, God knows. I was lucky to have had it full of health and effectiveness as long as I had. . . . I did not say, "Why me?" because the answer was so patently clear: "Why not me?"

AGNES DE MILLE

*D*id you think . . . that you needed, say, life? Do you think you will keep your life, or anything else you love? But no. . . . You see creatures die, and you know that you will die. And one day it occurs to you that you must not need life.

ANNIE DILLARD

This body
is my house—
it is not I.
Triumphant
in this faith
I live and die.

I don't know what will happen to me . . .
we've got some difficult days ahead,
but it doesn't matter to me now . . .
I've been to the mountain top . . .
Like anybody I'd like to live a long life . . .
But I'm not concerned about that now.
I just want to do God's will.
And he's allowed me to go up the mountain.
And I've looked over,
And I've seen the Promised Land.

MARTIN LUTHER KING, JR., speech to Memphis trashmen

*T*he salmon is still the swimmer in our language. . . .
They watched her last valiant fight for life, her struggle to
right herself when the gentle stream turned her, and they
watched the river force open her gills and draw her slowly
downstream, tail first, as she had started to the sea as a
fingerling . . . Mark saw that in Keetah's eyes there were
tears.

"It is always the same," she said. "The end of the
swimmer is sad."

"But, Keetah, it isn't. The whole life of the swimmer is
one of courage and adventure. All of it builds to the
climax and the end. When the swimmer dies he has spent
himself completely for the end which he has made, and this
is not sadness. It is triumph."

MARGARET CRAVEN, *I Heard the Owl Call My Name*

*N*ow, only memory   The reaching and the daring
Brings back the tempests   Were not your doing
Made by your reckless will   'Twas Nature
   Which pressed Life   In your
     itself   body
   To cry Halt   Too fiercely brewing.

WILLIAM J. RICE

*S*ome people confuse acceptance with apathy, but there's
all the difference in the world. Apathy fails to distinguish
between what can and cannot be helped; acceptance makes
that distinction. Apathy analyzes the will to action;
acceptance frees it by relieving it of impossible burdens.

ARTHUR GORDON

130

*H*ope claims the possibilities of the future, hopelessness recognizes its limits. In the mature person there are feelings of both, but they are kept distinct and separate. There's nothing wrong with hopeless feelings as long as they only limit, but do not contaminate the hope.

WILLIAM LYNCH

FALSE HOPE:	TRUE HOPE:
*I*f I permit only optimistic thoughts . . .	If I face both good and evil . . .
If I allow only positive feelings . . .	If I feel both fear and calm . . .
If I dream only possibility dreams . . .	If I live in the world as it is . . .
Then I can escape what has been	Then I can stand on what has been
And elude what might be.	And accept what may be.

Adapted from DAVID AUGSBURGER

O God, give us serenity to accept what cannot be changed; courage to change what should be changed, and wisdom to distinguish the one from the other.

REINHOLD NIEBUHR

*S*uffer us not to mock ourselves with falsehood
Teach us to care and not to care
Teach us to sit still
Even among these rocks,
Our peace in His will
And even among these rocks
Sister, mother
And spirit of the river, spirit of the sea,
Suffer me not to be separated

And let my cry come unto Thee.

T. S. ELIOT

*B*ut the painting selected by the judges for the first prize
was very different from all the others. It depicted the
height of a raging storm. Trees bent low under lashing
wind and driving rain. Lightning zigzagged across a
lowering, threatening sky. In the center of the fury the
artist had painted a bird's nest in the crotch of a gigantic
tree. There a mother bird spread her wings over her little
brood, waiting serene and unruffled until the storm would
pass. The painting was entitled very simply *Peace*.

CATHERINE MARSHALL

*M*y life flows on
An endless song
Above earth's lamentation
I hear the real though far-off hymn
That hails a new creation.

No storm can shake
My inmost calm
While to that Rock I'm clinging.
Since love is Lord of heaven
   and earth
How can I keep from singing?

FOLK SONG

*T*hose who have the strength and the love to sit with a dying patient in the *silence that goes beyond words* will know that this moment is neither frightening nor painful, but a peaceful cessation of the functioning of the body.
Watching a peaceful death of a human being reminds us of a falling star; one of the million lights in a vast sky that flares up for a brief moment only to disappear into the endless night forever.

ELISABETH KÜBLER-ROSS

I came in with Halley's Comet in 1835. It is coming again next year, and I expect to go out with it. It will be the greatest disappointment of my life if I don't go out with Halley's Comet. The Almighty has said, no doubt: "Now here are these two unaccountable freaks; they came in together, they must go out together."

MARK TWAIN, died April 21, 1910, the day after the perihelion of Halley's Comet

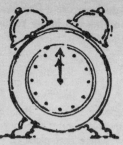

*Alarm clocks,
in parts of Africa,
are used as grave
decorations. They
are set at twelve
to wake the dead
on Judgment Day*

Very very slowly he dragged his right hand across his body to touch my hand. He was in terrible pain but he was still himself. . . . I remembered, while I sat and looked at him, that he had had one weakness: he had been afraid of thunder, and when a thunderstorm broke, while he was in my house, he adopted a rodent manner and looked round for a burrow. But here now he feared no more the lightning flash, nor the all-dreaded thunder-stone: he had plainly, I thought, done his worldly task, gone home. . . . If he were clear enough in his mind to look back at his life, he would find very few instances in which he had not got the better of it. A great vitality and power of enjoyment, a manifold activity were at their end here, where Kinanjui lay still. "Quiet consummation have, Kinanjui"—I thought.

ISAK DINESEN

One day I was alone with her. She was so sick and weak. I knew I had to do it soon. But how to do it? That was the question! How do I prepare a four-year-old child to die? She was lying on her bed in her room. I sat down next to her and said, "Cindy, I have something I want to tell you." She turned and looked at me with tears in her eyes. I said, "I know you have been feeling bad for quite a few months now. You can't play anymore; you can't go to nursery school anymore; you can't go to Sunday school anymore; you can't dance anymore. But there is a real special place you can go and pretty soon you will be going there. Do you know where that place is, Cindy?" She thought for a moment, then said "Heaven?" I said, "That's right!" Then I told her about all the people she would see there, all her little friends, and her grandparents. "They will be waiting for you," I told her. She had been listening very intently. Then, forcing back my own tears, I said, "But before you go to heaven, Cindy, you first have to die!" She just looked at me and said, "Oh, Mommy, I know that!" And I got the feeling she really *did* know and was now so glad that I knew too! It was no longer a secret that she had to keep. She seemed so relieved that she no longer had to protect me.

I saw a definite change in her after that. She became less agitated and seemed more comfortable. We talked a lot about heaven and about what she would shortly experience. She died four days later, and I am so glad now that I found the strength to do what I did. She seemed to experience a freedom upon discovering that at last I knew what she had apparently known for a long time.

RONALD J. KNAPP, quoting the mother of a four-year-old child with leukemia

*S*he closed her eyes; and in sweet slumber lying,
her spirit tiptoed from its lodging-place.
It's folly to shrink in fear, if this is dying;
        for death looked lovely in her lovely face.

PETRARCH

*W*ho are you,little i

(five or six years old)
peering from some high

window; at the gold

of november sunset

(and feeling:that if day
has to become night

this is a beautiful way)

e. e. cummings

*P*raise day at night, and life at the end.

GEORGE HERBERT

The crane—
Oriental "Bird of
Happiness"—
carries the soul
to the heavens.

MY SOUL AND I

As treading some long corridor,
  My soul and I together go;
Each day unlock another door
  To a new room we did not know.

And every night the darkness hides
  My soul from me awhile—but then
No fear nor loneliness abides;
  Hand clasped in hand, we wake again.

So when my soul and I, at last,
  Shall find but one dim portal more,
Shall we remembering all the past,
  Yet fear to try that other door?

CHARLES BUXTON GOING

We have been so long accustomed to the hypothesis of
your being taken away from us, especially during the past
ten months, that the thought that this may be your last
illness conveys no very sudden shock. You are old enough,
you've given your message to the world in many ways and
will not be forgotten; you are here left alone, and on the
other side, let us hope and pray, dear, dear old Mother is
waiting for you to join her. If you go, it will not be an
inharmonious thing. . . . As for the other side, and
Mother, and our all possibly meeting, I *can't* say anything.
More than ever at this moment do I feel that if that *were*
true, all would be solved and justified. And it comes
strangely over me in bidding you goodbye how a life is but
a day and expresses mainly but a single note. It is so much
like the act of bidding an ordinary good night. Good
night, my sacred old Father! If I don't see you again—
Farewell! a blessed farewell!

WILLIAM JAMES, letter to his father, Henry James, Sr.,
during the latter's final illness

Death,—a passage outside the range of imagination, but within the range of experience.

ISAK DINESEN

Each day is a little life; every waking and rising a little birth, every fresh morning a little youth, every going to rest and sleep a little death.

ARTHUR SCHOPENHAUER

Death is a night that lies between two days—the day of life on earth and the day of eternal life in the world to come.

MAURICE LAMM

Sleep is a death; O, wake me try, by sleeping what it is
    to die,
And as gently lay my head on my grave, as now my bed.

SIR THOMAS BROWNE

Sleep on in thy beauty,
  Thou sweet angel
    child,
By sorrow unslighted,
  By sin undefiled.

Like the dove to the ark,
  Thou hast flown to
    the rest,
From the wild sea of strife,
  To the home of the blest.

MOURNING CARD of James S. Pilling, died at age 8, 1889

*W*ould I bring her back to life if I could do it? I would not. If a word would do it, I would beg for strength to withhold the word. And I would have the strength; I am sure of it. In her loss I am almost bankrupt, and my life is a bitterness, but I am content: for she has been enriched with that most precious of all gifts—that gift which makes all other gifts mean and poor—death. I have never wanted any released friend of mine restored to life since I reached manhood. I felt in this way when Susy passed away; and later my wife, and later Mr. Rogers. When Clara met me at the station in New York and told me Mr. Rogers had died suddenly that morning, my thought was, Oh, favorite of fortune—fortunate all his long and lovely life—fortunate to his latest moment! The reporters said there were tears of sorrow in my eyes. True—but they were for *me*, not for him. He had suffered no loss. All the fortunes he had ever made before were poverty compared with this one.

MARK TWAIN

*D*one crossed every river,
Done reached this one;
Now I know my crossin's done.
Hallelujah, Lord, your rest feel good.
Hallelujah, Lord, your rest feel good.

OWEN DOBSON

*H*e has outsoared the shadow of our night;
Envy and calumny and hate and pain,
And that unrest which men miscall delight
Can touch him not and torture not again;
From the contagion of the world's slow stain
He is secure, and now can never mourn
A heart grown cold, a head grown grey in vain.

PERCY BYSSHE SHELLEY

*D*eath is in my sight today
As when a man desires to see home
When he has spent many years in captivity.

The Man Who Was Tired of Life, c. 1990 B.C.

On the soul's
journey to his
next life, he is
nourished by
the great
"Heart berry"

—CHIPPEWA INDIAN LEGEND

*B*ut the Jerusalem above is free; she is our mother.

GALATIANS 4:26

I saw battle-corpses, myriads of them,
And the white skeletons of young men, I saw them,
I saw the debris and debris of all the slain soldiers of
   the war,
But I saw they were not as was thought,
They themselves were fully at rest, they suffer'd not,
The living remain'd and suffer'd, the mother suffer'd,
And the wife and the child and the musing comrade
   suffer'd,
And the armies that remain'd suffer'd.

WALT WHITMAN

*R*eason thus with life:
If I do lose thee, I do lose a thing
That none but fools would keep.

WILLIAM SHAKESPEARE

*A*h! Vanitas vanitatum! Which of us is happy in this
world? Which of us has his desire? Or, having it, is
satisfied?—Come, children, let us shut up the box and the
puppets, for our play is played out.

WILLIAM MAKEPEACE THACKERAY

*I*f we were immortal we should all be miserable; no doubt
it is hard to die, but it is sweet to think that we shall not
live for ever, and that a better life will put an end to the
sorrows of this world. If we had the offer of immortality
here below, who would accept the sorrowful gift?

JEAN-JACQUES ROUSSEAU, *Emile*

*T*he modern philosopher had told me again and again that I was in the right place, and I had still felt depressed even in acquiescence. But I had heard that I was in the wrong place, and my soul sang for joy, like a bird in spring.

G. K. CHESTERTON

*W*hile we are aspiring towards our true country, we be pilgrims on earth.

JOHN CALVIN

*W*e have not always been or will not always be purely temporal creatures. . . . Not only are we harried by time, we seem unable, despite a thousand generations, even to get used to it. We are always amazed at it—how fast it goes, how slowly it goes, how much of it is gone. Where, we cry, has the time gone? We aren't adapted to it, not at home in it. If that is so, it may appear as a proof, or at least a powerful suggestion, that eternity exists and is our home. . . .

SHELDON VANAUKEN

*H*ere lies a poor woman who was always tired,
She lived in a house where help wasn't hired:
Her last words on earth were: "Dear friends, I am going
To where there's no cooking, or washing, or sewing—
Don't mourn for me now, don't mourn for me never,
I am going to do nothing for ever and ever."

ANONYMOUS

*N*o one knows whether death, which men in their fear apprehend to be the greatest evil, may not be the greatest good.

PLATO

A dialogue between two infants in the womb concerning the state of this world, might handsomely illustrate our ignorance of the next.

SIR THOMAS BROWNE

*L*ife is a great surprise. I do not see why death should not be an even greater one.

VLADIMIR NABOKOV

*T*he sight of stars always sets me dreaming just as naively as those black dots on a map set me dreaming of towns and villages. Why should those points of light in the firmament, I wonder, be less accessible than the dark ones on the map of France? We take a train to go to Tarascon or Rouen and we take death to go to a star.

VINCENT VAN GOGH, referring to his painting, "The Starry Night"

Death is only a horizon; and a horizon is nothing save the limit of our sight.

ROSSITER WORTHINGTON RAYMOND

I never saw a Moor—
I never saw the Sea—
Yet know I how the
    Heather looks
And what a
    Billow be.

I never spoke with God
Nor visited in Heaven—
Yet certain am I of
    the spot
As if the Checks were
    given

EMILY DICKINSON

*W*hen the great chemist, Sir Faraday, was on his deathbed, some journalists questioned him as to his speculations concerning the soul and death. "Speculations!" said the dying man in astonishment, "I know nothing about speculations, I am resting on certainties."

MRS. CHARLES E. COWMAN

*"M*y life is drawing to a close. I know that, I feel it. But I also feel every day that is left to me how my earthly life is already in touch with a new, infinite, unknown but fast approaching future life, the anticipation of which sets my soul trembling with rapture, and my mind glowing, and my heart weeping with joy."

FYODOR DOSTOEVSKY, *The Brothers Karamazov*

*W*ill the circle be unbroken?
By and by, Lord, by and by
There's a better home a-waitin'
In the sky, Lord, in the sky.

FOLK SONG

I saw eternity
the other night
like a great ring
of pure and
endless light.

—HENRY VAUGHAN

On earth the broken arcs; in heaven, a perfect round.

ROBERT BROWNING

I was never afraid of Hell, nor never grew pale at the description of that place; I have so fixed my contemplations on Heaven, that I have almost forgot the Idea of Hell, and am afraid rather to lose the Joys of the one, than endure the misery of the other. . . .

SIR THOMAS BROWNE, *Religio Medici*

146

Come now, thou greatest of feasts on the journey to
    freedom eternal;
Death, cast aside all the burdensome chains, and demolish
The walls of our temporal body, the walls of our souls that
    are blinded,
So that at last we may see that which here remains hidden.
Freedom, how long we have sought thee in discipline,
    action and suffering;
Dying, we now may behold thee revealed in the Lord.

DIETRICH BONHOEFFER

Oh! I have slipped the surly bonds of earth
And danced the skies on laughter-silvered wings . . .
And, while with silent, lifting mind I've trod
The high untrespassed sanctity of space,
Put out my hand and touched the face of God.

JOHN GILLESPIE MAGEE, JR.

Suddenly her fingers tightened on mine. She said in a clear
weak voice: "Oh, dearling, look. . . ." She didn't go on,
if there was more. I *knew* that if I said, "What is it?" she
would make an effort and go on; but I did not do so. I
don't know why I didn't. She might have been saying,
"look," as one who suddenly understands something, or as
one who beholds—what? . . . And I shall not know this
side of eternity, for they were her last words: "Oh,
dearling, look!"

SHELDON VANAUKEN

*A*nd I saw a new heaven and a new earth. . . . I, John, saw the holy city, new Jerusalem, coming down from God out of heaven, prepared as a bride adorned for her husband. . . . And the city had no need of the sun, neither of the moon, to shine in it: for the glory of God did lighten it. . . .

REVELATION 21:1–2,23

The dolphin — considered to be the strongest fish and believed to be the carrier of the soul across the waters to the world beyond.

*T*here are more things in heaven and earth, Horatio, than are dreamt of in your philosophy.

WILLIAM SHAKESPEARE, *Hamlet*

*I*n this mode of perception, biological death can be understood as the annihilation of the final set of barriers between man and God, and as the Supreme achievement of transcendence. Time does not matter here: "Before Abraham was," said Jesus, "I Am."

SANDOL STODDARD

One gets glimpses, even in our country, of that which is ageless—heavy thought in the face of an infant, and frolic childhood in that of a very old man. Here it was all like that.

C. S. LEWIS, *The Great Divorce*

i am a little church(no great cathedral)
far from the splendor and squalor of hurrying cities
—i do not worry if briefer days grow briefest,
i am not sorry when sun and rain make april

my life is the life of the reaper and the sower;
my prayers are prayers of earth's own clumsily striving
(finding and losing and laughing and crying)children
whose any sadness or joy is my grief or my gladness

around me surges a miracle of unceasing
birth and glory and death and resurrection:
over my sleeping self float flaming symbols
of hope, and i wake to a perfect patience of mountains

i am a little church(far from the frantic
world with its rapture and anguish)at peace with nature
—i do not worry if longer nights grow longest;
i am not sorry when silence becomes singing

winter by spring, i lift my diminutive spire to
merciful Him Whose only now is forever:
standing erect in the deathless truth of His presence
(welcoming humbly His light and proudly His darkness)

e. e. cummings

From what we are told by most of those who have reported such incidents, the moment of death can be one of unparalleled beauty, peace and comfort—a feeling of total love and total acceptance. This is possible even for those involved in horrible accidents in which they suffered very serious injuries. To me, there is a tremendous comfort potential here for people who are facing death, as obviously we all are.

DR. KENNETH RING

"Do not let your hearts be troubled. Trust in God; trust also in me. In my Father's house are many rooms; if it were not so, I would have told you. I am going to prepare a place for you."

.   .   .   .

For our homeland is in heaven, and from heaven comes the Savior we are waiting for, the Lord Jesus Christ, who, by the power that enables him to bring everything under his control, will transform our lowly bodies so that they will be like his glorious body.

JOHN 14:1–4, PHILIPPIANS 3:20–21

Being "glorified"—I know the meaning of that now. It's the time, after my death here, when I'll be dancing on my feet.

JONI EARECKSON TADA, paralyzed from the neck down in a diving accident

I shall hear in Heaven.

LUDWIG VAN BEETHOVEN, last words

*T*he body of
Benjamin Franklin, Printer,
Like the cover of an old book,
Its contents torn out,
And stript of its lettering and gilding,
Lies here, food for worms,
But the work shall not be lost,
For it will, as he believ'd,
Appear once more
In a new and more elegant edition,
Corrected and improved
By the Author

BENJAMIN FRANKLIN, epitaph he wrote for his gravestone

I come to tell news
I come to tell news
The buffaloes are coming again
The buffaloes are coming again
My father tells
The Dead People are coming again
The Dead People are coming again
My father tells
The earth will be made new
The earth will be made new
Says the mother.

GHOST DANCE of the Plains Indians

"Oh Lord. Almighty God. Hit ain't for us ignorant mortals to say what's right and what's wrong. Was any one of us to be a-doin' of it, we'd not of brung this pore boy into the world a cripple, and his mind teched. We'd of brung him in straight and tall like his brothers, fitten to live and work and do. But in a way o' speakin', Lord, you done made it up to him. You give him a way with the wild creeturs. You give him a sort o' wisdom, made him knowin' and gentle. The birds come to him, and the varmints moved free about him, and like as not he could o' takened a she wild-cat right in his pore twisted hands.

"Now you've done seed fit to take him where bein' crookedy in mind or limb don't matter. But Lord, hit pleasures us to think now you've done straightened out them legs and that pore bent back and them hands. Hit pleasures us to think on him, movin' around as easy as any one. And Lord, give him a few red-birds and mebbe a squirrel and a 'coon and a 'possum to keep him comp'ny, like he had here. All of us is somehow lonesome, and we know he'll not be lonesome, do he have them leetle wild things around him, if it ain't askin' too much to put a few varmints in Heaven. Thy will be done. Amen."

MARJORIE KINNAN RAWLINGS, *The Yearling*

God forbid that I should go to any heaven in which there are no horses.

ROBERT BONTINE CUNNINGHAME-GRAHAM, letter to Theodore Roosevelt

When his earthly work is done,
Look kindly on the work nut.
And in heaven's pasture, Lord,
Leave a little grass to cut.

PATRICIA S. RUTTER

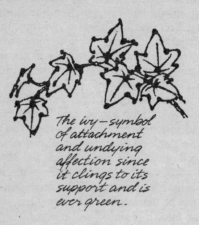

The ivy — symbol of attachment and undying affection since it clings to its support and is ever green.

Here lie I, Martin Elginbrodde:
Have mercy on my soul, Lord God,
As I would do, were I Lord God
and You were Martin Elginbrodde.

EPITAPH in Elgin Cathedral

*M*an does not possess an indestructible spirit that will never die. The human body is a psychosomatic unity (*psyche*—soul; *soma*—body), and as such is subject to death. The entire human being dies, and the entire human being is given a new bodily existence by God in the resurrection of the dead. The resurrection of the dead is God's gift; it is in no way an inherent capacity of the human being.

THE REV. FLEMING RUTLEDGE

*B*e comforted; it is not from yourself that you must expect it, but on the contrary, you must expect it by expecting nothing from yourself.

BLAISE PASCAL

AMAZING GRACE

*A*mazing grace! how sweet the sound
That saved a wretch like me!
I once was lost, but now am found,
Was blind, but now I see.

'Twas grace that taught my heart to fear,
And grace my fears relieved;
How precious did that grace appear
The hour I first believed!

Through many dangers, toils and snares
I have already come;
It's grace that brought me safe thus far
And grace will lead me home.

When we've been there ten thousand years,
Bright shining as the sun,
We've no less days to sing God's praise
Than when we first begun.

JOHN NEWTON

God's purpose is not death, but resurrection.

THE REVEREND ROSS WRIGHT

God loves more than the molecules that happen to be in the body at the time of death. He loves a body that is marked by all the tribulation and also the ceasing longing of a pilgrimage. . . . Resurrection of the body means that none of this is lost to God, since he loves man. He has gathered together old dreams and not a single smile has escaped his notice. Resurrection of the body means that man rediscovers not only his last moment but his history.

WILHELM BRUENING

I was once a sinner man,
Living unsaved and wild,
Taking my chances in a dangerous world,
Putting my soul on trial.
Because of Your mercy,
Falling down on me like rain,
Because of Your mercy,
When I die I'll live again.

MAYA ANGELOU

*O*ur Lord has written the promise of resurrection,
not in books alone, but in every leaf of springtime.

MARTIN LUTHER

*Y*ou cannot tell the unhappy person that he or she has
nothing to worry about because at the end of life he will
become absorbed in some kind of collective
Unconscious. . . . What sort of a God would it be who
would absorb us into Himself and snuff out our own
individuality in the process? . . . Life either has meaning
for me, for my own personal speck of cosmic dust
existence, or it has no meaning at all.

ANDREW GREELEY

*T*his is really not so difficult to understand. Scientists tell us that the body is constantly wearing away and reproducing itself. . . . the actual atoms that make up our body now are different from those in our body four or five years ago. And the substance of the soft parts is completely exchanged every few months. Yet we know that our body is the identical one we had last year.

Perhaps the same thing will be true of our resurrected bodies. We do not know the chemical composition of that body, but. . . . it will be just as much our body as our body today is the one we had a year ago. It will be our body because it will be perfectly suited to us and to our spirit.

KENNETH S. KANTZER

*H*eaven and Earth are threads from one loom.

ANONYMOUS BROTHER of the Shaker faith

*F*or there is nothing ever lost
or eternally neglected,
For everything God ever made
Is always resurrected;

So trust God's all-wise wisdom
and doubt the Father never,
For in His heavenly kingdom
There is nothing lost forever.

HELEN STEINER RICE

A rose will still be a rose in heaven, it will just smell ten times sweeter.

—PEGGY WOODSON

ON MY CHILD'S DEATH

Clocks strike in the
    distance,
Already the night grows
    late,
How dimly the lamp
    glistens;
Your bed is all made.

It is the wind goes,
    only,
Grieving around the house;
Where, inside, we sit lonely
Often listening out.

It is as if, how
    lightly,
You must be going to
    knock,
Had missed your way and
    might be
Tired, now, coming back.

We are poor, poor stupid
    folk!
It's we, still lost in dread,
Who wander in the dark—
You've long since found
    your bed.

JOSEPH VON EICHENDORF

159

She is with me, as real as the winter snow that blends the tears upon my face. And it is only when I try to touch her, to make her linger yet awhile, that she dies all over again.

SAMANTHA MOONEY

Remember me when I am gone away,
Gone far away into the silent land;
When you can no more hold me by the hand,
Nor I half turn to go, yet turning stay.

Yet if you should forget me for a while
And afterwards remember, do not grieve:
For if the darkness and corruption leave
A vestige of the thoughts that once I had, ·
Better by far you should forget and smile
than that you should remember and be sad.

CHRISTINA ROSSETTI

The goal is to strike that delicate balance between the past that should be remembered and a future that must be created.

EARL A. GROLLMAN

Peace; come away: the song of woe
    Is after all an earthly song.
    Peace; come away: we do him wrong
To sing so wildly: let us go.

ALFRED, LORD TENNYSON

*D*o you know what the last words she spoke to me were? She opened her great big, wondrous Italian eyes, and saw me with tears running down my cheeks and she said— imagine this—"Felice, what are you holding on to?"

LEO F. BUSCAGLIA

*M*ama has died. I am left with all the good she did for me and all the bad I did to her.

ALEXANDER SOLZHENITSYN

*M*issing him now, I am haunted by my own shortcomings, how often I failed him. I think every parent must have a sense of failure, even of sin, merely in remaining alive after the death of a child. One feels that it is not right to live when one's child has died, that one should somehow have found the way to give one's life to save his life. Failing there, one's failures during his too brief life seem all the harder to bear and forgive. . . .

I wish we had loved Johnny more when he was alive. Of course we loved Johnny very much. Johnny knew that. Everybody knew it. Loving Johnny more. What does it mean? What can it mean, now?

FRANCES GUNTHER, excerpt from JOHN GUNTHER's memoir of their son

"*I*f only," he said—two words with which all who have lost a loved one must come to terms.

JANE BURGESS KOHN

I was not at her bedside
that final day, I did not grant her ancient,
huge-knuckled hand
its last wish, I did not let it
gradually become empty of the son's hand—and so
hand her, with more steadiness, into the future.

. . . .

I know now there are regrets
we can never be rid of;
permanent remorse. Knowing this, I know also
I am to draw from that surplus stored up
of tenderness which was hers by right,
and which no one ever gave her,
and give it away, freely.

GALWAY KINNELL

*I*n the early 1970s I counseled many young men returning
to college after combat in Vietnam. I was astonished at
how many of these men felt guilty for coming home alive.
As one highly decorated soldier put it, "I knew and loved
better men than me who died there."

In almost every situation it is outside the realm of
anybody's power to determine which persons live or die.
You need not impose on yourself a penalty for your own
life and health and good fortune simply because others
suffer terribly. We can live useful lives in appreciation of
our own health and continuing existence. No more than
that is required of us.

ANN KAISER STERNS, *Living Through Personal Crisis*

"The heart's affections are divided like the branches of the cedar tree; if the tree loses one strong branch, it will suffer but it does not die. It will pour all its vitality into the next branch so that it will grow and fill the empty space." This is what your mother told me when her father died, and you should say the same thing when death takes my body to its resting place and my soul to God's care.

KAHLIL GIBRAN, *The Broken Wings*

The cedar tree —
symbol of strength,
new life and growth

I have often heard such criticisms leveled at widows and widowers who; instead of sinking into gloom, remain active and serene.

I think there is a certain amount of psychological over-compensation in my present activity, and in my writing so many books. All my work, in any case, could be interpreted as a "work of mourning." But I find in it a sort of fellowship with Nelly: we did everything together, and in a way we still do. I have a strong sense of her invisible spirit. . . . There are widowers who, as it were, suspend their lives, as if life had stopped at the moment of their bereavement. Their present thoughts have turned toward the past, whereas I live in the present and look to the future.

For some, therefore, it is, if anything, a retrograde and paralyzing presence, whereas my wife's presence is living and stimulating.

PAUL TOURNIER

*A*m I healing? I'm able to gaze at her photograph without that tourniquet tightening around my throat, clamping memory. . . .
I'm beginning to see her in *her* life, and not only myself bereft of her life. . . .
. . . .
Piece by piece, I reenter the world. A new phase. A new body, a new voice. Birds console me by flying, trees by growing, dogs by the warm patch they leave behind on the sofa. Unknown people merely by performing their motions. It's like a slow recovery from a sickness, this recovery of one's self. . . . My mother was at peace. She was ready. A free woman. "Let me go," she said. Okay, Mama. I'm letting you go.

TOBY TALBOT

164

I will turn to her as often as possible in gladness. I will even salute her with a laugh. The less I mourn her the nearer I seem to her.

C. S. LEWIS

OLD BURIAL HILL,
MARBLEHEAD, MASSACHUSETTS

Give joy or grief give ease
    or pain
Take life and friends
    away
But let me find them all
    again
In the eternal day

In remembrance of 3 daughters of
Jones and Sarah Dennis
1781, 1792, 1802

Happy Infant early
    blessed,
Rest in peaceful slumber,
    rest
Early rescu'd from the
    cares,
Which increase with
    growing years.

In memory of Benjamin Selman,
May 17, 1802,
2 years, 28 days old

Friends nor physicians,
    cannot save,
My mortal body from the
    grave,
Nor can the grave confine
    me here,
When Jesus calls me to
    appear.

In memory of Mr. William
Humphreys,
April 10, 1811, Age 23

Hope looks beyond the
    bonds of time,
When what we now
    deplore,
Shall rise in full immortal
    prime,
And bloom to fade no
    more.

In memory of Mary Owens Dodd,
October 15, 1825, Age 15

Farewell to earth and
   welcome to the skies,
In yonder world see the
   bright star arise,
She now has left the
   cumbrous clods of clay,
And soars triumphant to the
   realms of day.
Gone to behold her Saviour
   and Her God,
O may we tread the blissful
   path she trod.

In memory of Mrs. Elizabeth Huler,
June 24, 1815

'Tis thro my Saviour's blood
   alone
I look for mercy at thy
   throne
I leave the world without a
   tear
Save for the friends I hold so
   dear
To heal their sorrows Lord
   descend
And to the friendless prove a
   friend.

In memory of Mary A. Brown,
August 30, 1827, Age 44

GOODNIGHT, WILLIE LEE, I'LL SEE YOU IN THE MORNING

*L*ooking down into my father's
dead face
for the last time
my mother said without
tears, without smiles
without regrets
but with *civility*
"Goodnight, Willie Lee, I'll see you
in the morning."
And it was then I knew that the healing
of all our wounds
is forgiveness
that permits a promise
of our return
at the end.

ALICE WALKER

*S*he said not "good-bye" but "forgive me". . . . the two words (in Russian) are practically interchangeable! It is the profoundest, the last good-bye.

ANNE MORROW LINDBERGH

A small boy's dog was killed by an automobile. His first reaction was one of shock and dismay, followed by outrage against his parents. He felt they were guilty because they had not taken proper care of the pet. (The boy behaved like an adult who rages against God for neglecting His charges.) Yet anger against the parents was a substitute for his own guilt, for the youngster had on occasion wished to be rid of "that awful pest." The child insisted that one of his favorite toys be buried with the dog. The toy served as a kind of peace offering to the offended pet. Now the lad was freed of anxiety and could continue to function effectively in his everyday activities. Ritual combined the dynamics of guilt, assuagement, and reparation—similar to the mourning behavior of adults.

EARL A. GROLLMAN

*M*y heart was heavy, for its trust had been
Abused, its Kindness answered with foul wrong:
So, turning gloomily from my fellow-men,
One summer Sabbath-day, I strolled among
The green mounds of the village burial place;
Where, pondering how all human love and hate
Find one sad level, and how, soon or late,
Wronged and wrongdoer, each with meekened face
And cold hands folded over a still heart,
Pass the green threshold of our common grave,
Wither all footsteps tend, whence none depart,
Awed for myself and pitying my race,
Our common sorrow, like a mighty wave,
Swept all my pride away, and, trembling, I forgave.

JOHN GREENLEAF WHITTIER

*L*et Jew and Gentile, meeting
From many a distant shore,
Around one altar kneeling,
One common Lord adore.
Let all that now divides us
Remove and pass away,
Like shadows of the morning
Before the blaze of day

HENRY SMART

*A*nd throughout all eternity
I forgive you, you forgive me.

WILLIAM BLAKE

*W*hen Bill was admitted I sensed his anger. He was hostile and abrupt. And very restless. When he finally fell asleep he would moan as if something terribly wrong had happened.

I asked him if everything was O.K. He didn't answer. So I asked again. No response. It was then that I knew he had some unfinished business that needed to be completed if he was to die a good death.

His physical signs were rapidly deteriorating. But he wouldn't die. He wouldn't let go. It was as if there was something deep within him that would not permit death.

I talked to his son: "Something very deep is bothering your dad. I don't know what it is. But unless it is resolved your father will never die in peace."

The son's eyes filled with tears. The family secret was about to be told.

"I am not the only child. I have a sister who lives in Baltimore, Maryland. My dad disowned her nine years ago because she married someone of another race. From his point of view, she committed the unpardonable sin. He said he would never forgive her."

When I heard that confession I knew what his unfinished business was all about. I told the son to call his sister and tell her to get to Minneapolis as fast as possible.

Five hours later she arrived. I went with them to their father's room. For the first time in nine years he saw his daughter. He said nothing but just stared at her. Then he opened his arms to his daughter and with all the strength that was left in that frail body hugged her. She brushed away his tears and sat on the bed. They said nothing for the longest time.

Finally he looked into her eyes and said two words that freed him forever: "I'm sorry."

There were many tears. They held one another and talked about old times. The dad learned that he was a grandfather and there was much laughter.

I checked his vital signs later that evening and they seemed stronger. But then an amazing thing happened.

Around 10:30 P.M. the father said that he was very

tired. But he didn't want the children to leave the room. I sensed what was about to happen and told the son and daughter to stay.

Each child held his hand. And then he died. But his expression was serene. The bitterness was gone. Grievances had been resolved. All unfinished business put to rest.

ROBERT VENINGA

It is important that when we come to die we have nothing to do but to die.

CHARLES HODGE

There is a kind of release
And a kind of torment in every goodbye
for every man.

C. DAY LEWIS

This is the Hour of lead—
Remembered, if outlived,
As Freezing—persons, recollect the Snow—
First—Chill—then Stupor—then the letting go.

EMILY DICKINSON

You have grown wings of pain
and flap around the bed like a wounded gull
calling for water, calling for tea, for grapes
whose skins you cannot penetrate.
Remember when you taught me
how to swim? Let go, you said,
the lake will hold you up.
I long to say, Father let go
and death will hold you up . . .

LINDA PASTAN

One does not discover new lands without consenting to
lose sight of the shore . . .

ANDRÉ GIDE

*S*unset and evening star,
    And one clear call for me!
And may there be no moaning of the bar,
    When I put out to sea,

But such a tide as moving seems asleep,
    Too full for sound and foam,
When that which drew from out the boundless deep
    Turns again home.

Twilight and evening bell,
    And after that the dark!
And may there be no sadness of farewell,
    When I embark;

For tho' from out our bourne of Time and Place
    The flood may bear me far,
I hope to see my Pilot face to face
    When I have crost the bar.

ALFRED, LORD TENNYSON

*T*he door is open wide, Marcy
So let your sorrows fly
On the wings of a song
That you've sung your whole life long
Song of your heart-in-flight
Come on home to the light
Home, like a folding of wings

CRIS WILLIAMSON

*Still around
the corner
there may wait
A new road,
or a secret gate.*

Turn up the lights. I don't want to go home in the dark.

O. HENRY, last words

If I of Heaven may have my fill, Take thou the world, and all that will.

ANN BRADSTREET

A mighty fortress is our
   God
A bulwark never failing;
Our helper He amid the
   flood
Of mortal ills prevailing.

Let goods and kindred
   go,
This mortal life also;
The body they may
   kill:
God's truth abideth still;
His kingdom is forever.

MARTIN LUTHER

*E*very parting gives a foretaste of death; every coming together again a foretaste of the resurrection.

ARTHUR SCHOPENHAUER

*T*he coach is at the door at last;
The eager children, mounting fast
And kissing hands, in chorus sing:
Goodbye, goodbye, to everything!
To house and garden, field and lawn,
The meadow-gates we swung upon,
To pump and stable, tree and swing,
Goodbye, goodbye, to everything!

And fare you well for evermore,
O ladder at the hayloft door,
O hayloft where the cobwebs cling,
Goodbye, goodbye, to everything!
Crack goes the whip, and off we go;
The trees and houses smaller grow;
Last, round the woody turn we swing;
Goodbye, goodbye, to everything!

ROBERT LOUIS STEVENSON

*"N*ight is drawing nigh—"
For all that has been—Thanks!
To all that shall be—Yes!

DAG HAMMARSKJÖLD

ABOUT THE EDITORS

Gail Perry is an art designer in San Francisco who is most skilled in the ability to enliven poetry and prose with effective layout and imagery. Her deep appreciation for literature, coupled with her faith in a God who offers fullness of life on earth and hope for life after death, resulted in the concept behind *A Rumor of Angels*.

Gail's sister, Jill Perry, works with "special needs" children in Boston. She was previously an occupational therapist, a teacher and a family service worker in the Appalachian Mountains. Jill has consistently involved herself in the hardship of her patients, students and clients; she is convinced that to share pain and to encourage hope is to love.

A revelation inducing
new insight or inspiration . . .
addressing issues that confront us
individually and collectively . . .

BALLATINE/ EPIPHANY